~ Shifting and Shenanigans ~

Magical Mystery Book Club, 1

By Elizabeth Pantley

www.ElizabethPantley.com

With special thanks to Robert, Linda,
Nick, Mia, and Thomas

Cover Design by
Molly Burton, Cozy Cover Designs
https://cozycoverdesigns.com

Editing by Melissa Bowersock

Disclaimer

Table of Contents

1

I pulled the soft blanket all the way up to my nose and sunk into my cozy loveseat. Hah. Loveseat was a terrible name for the one piece of furniture I chose to keep when I moved out of our home. Well, Spencer's parent's rental home. It wasn't 'our' anything anymore. My husband Spencer – I mean, as of today, my ex-husband Spencer told me I could keep whatever I wanted. He didn't care. That was the core problem with Spencer. He didn't care. About anything.

The failure of our relationship wasn't really his fault. When we met in college, I was far too busy to notice that he was devoid of any real personality. We spent our evenings studying and our weekends out with friends. When we graduated everyone assumed that we'd marry. So, we did. On my first anniversary I wondered how many years we'd be together before we got divorced.

Seven. That's how many years. I never would have guessed we'd make it that far. I figured he would have bored me to death way before then. Luckily, we had agreed to put off starting a family until we 'found ourselves.' Since we never did find ourselves, we never did start that family.

I hit the remote and scanned the channels for a movie. I skipped over every love story and settled into watching old episodes of *Friends*. Joey was piling on all of Chandler's clothes to get back at him for hiding all his underwear and forcing him to go commando. I'd seen this episode a dozen times, but when Joey says he's even now going commando it still made me laugh. I was so engrossed in my comforting group of TV friends that I didn't even hear the front door open.

"Hel-loooo! Paige?"

"Hey, Glo. In here watching TV."

Her cheerful voice lifted my spirits. My Aunt Gloria was my best friend. Some people might think that's a bit weird, but she was nine years younger than my mom, and way more fun than my overly serious mother. She'd always been my go-to person when Mom got on my case for some reason or other. And that was often. My mother was a serious person, and I ... was not. Glo was a perpetual optimist and never ceased to lighten my mood. Over the years she'd become much more friend than aunt, and over time she'd instructed me to drop the 'aunt' which she said was implied.

I heard her go in and out the door twice, and then I heard her rustling about, bumping into things, and glasses clinking. Finally, she came into the room juggling two glasses and a bottle of champagne.

"Look what I brought! It's not every day a girl turns thirty the same day her divorce is final. Happy Birthday and Happy ... umm ... Happy Independence Day!" Her unrestrained laughter never failed to bring a smile to my face. She loved life, my joyful aunt, and she never turned down a chance for happiness.

I took the glasses from her and set them on the coffee table. Then the two of us made a mockery of suave champagne bottle opening and managed to spill it all over the floor. We cleaned up our mess and filled our glasses, then made a toast to Independence Day.

Glo took a sip then scurried out of the room. She came back holding a large gift-wrapped present and placed it on the floor in front of me.

"Go ahead! Open it," she said as she plopped down on the sofa next to me.

I tore through the paper to find an unusual

assortment of items. A snorkel set, a pair of horse stirrups, a yoga mat, a vegetarian cookbook, and a cat toy were among the odd gifts.

"See? Whatever do you need Spencer for? Now you have the freedom to do all the good stuff in life." She leaned over and gave me a one-armed hug, her other hand raising her champagne glass in the air. "Cheers!"

I tapped my glass to hers. "Thank you so much, Glo! You're a bit crazy though. What is all this?"

"Your happiness is your own responsibility, Paige. Now that Spencer is out of your life, you'll have the ability to capture all those fun dreams you had, but never did anything about. Scuba diving, horseback riding lessons, yoga classes. And you can finally give vegetarianism a try, since you won't be cooking beef and chicken every night. It's time to start working on your own peace and contentment instead of always catering to a husband who doesn't appreciate – or even care about – everything you do for him."

I held up a colorful silk monogrammed scarf with the letters PE in beautiful script lettering. A smile lit my face.

"You don't have to be Paige Turner anymore. No more ignoring people's snickers when you introduce yourself. You can go back to being Paige Erickson."

I laughed and blushed. "I already have the paperwork filled out!"

I decided that I didn't want to talk about Spencer anymore. I picked up a toy F-250 pickup truck. "And what exactly is this?"

"Inspiration for your road trip around the mountains of Colorado!" She raised her hand. "I volunteer to do that one with you!"

"Well since you're the one with the truck, I guess you'll have to." I reached into the box and pulled out a cat toy. My insides did a happy little dance, and I tilted my head at her.

"I know you've always wanted a cat, and now that Mr. Allergic is gone you can get one!"

"What a great idea," I said, shaking the cat toy and making it jingle.

"Now, what is this?" I pulled out a large manila envelope that was at the bottom of the box.

"Let's refill our glasses first. I have some sad news, first. But then I have great news."

~ ~ ~

Glo decided we should make a tray of appetizers to go along with our champagne before she shared her news. We dug through my cabinets and refrigerator and put together a tasty mix of fruits, crackers, cheese, olives, and pretzels. Glo even added some leftover Chinese food to the mix.

I settled into my favorite spot on the not-such-a-loveseat. Glo filled our glasses with more champagne. Instead of sitting in the chair that she usually occupied she plunked herself down next to me and took my hands in hers.

"There's no gentle way to tell you this, so I'm just going to come out and say it. GeeGee passed away."

"What?! When? How could she die?"

"Honey, your great-grandmother was ninety-one."

"But last time I saw her – just months ago! – she was full of energy and vibrant health!"

Glo sucked in a deep breath. "I was told that she drowned."

"Drowned! How could that happen?"

"She was out on a fishing boat with a friend, and she fell overboard. They were out in the middle of the lake. They never found her—"

"What was she doing *fishing*? I don't think she's ever fished before in her life!"

"You know your GeeGee. She was always up for a new experience. Paige, she had a very full, happy life."

"That doesn't help." I could feel the tears filling my eyes, and my throat tightened. I tried to swallow. I love – *loved* – my great-grandmother. When I was growing up, I spent several weeks every summer with her at her small inn just five hours away from us in Cascade Valley. She was so much like Glo – a happy, dynamic woman who filled the world with joy. I hadn't seen her as much as I liked over the past seven years because Spencer said her energy and quirkiness gave him a headache. I suddenly missed her so much it hurt. I wrapped my arms around my stomach and let the tears fall. Glo wrapped her arms around me and I felt her own tears mix with mine.

Through our sorrow we began to share our favorite memories of GeeGee and her homey inn.

"Remember how she named the Snapdragon Inn?" Glo asked, and our tears turned to giggles.

"That was the year I was a dinosaur- and dragon-crazy preschooler," I laughed. "I wanted her to name it the Tetradactyl Inn, but she came up with Snapdragon. She invented a new dragon by that name and told me all about it. It was the largest dragon ever discovered, and it breathed fire. Oddly, it was a gentle herbivore. It wasn't until I was twelve that I learned it was the name of a flower."

Glo and I shared GeeGee stories while we snacked our way through the tray of food. Eventually buoyed by happy memories, the pain began to lessen. We cleaned up the dishes and made a pot of tea, then curled up on our seats. Glo had the large envelope from my gift box in her hand.

"It's time for the great news!" she announced fluttering the envelope at me. "This is GeeGee's will."

"Glo, I wouldn't call that great news." I frowned.

"GeeGee has a note tacked on the front of the envelope. Look. She pointed to the small note and read it out loud. 'Glo and Paige, this is great news and I want you to take it that way. No fancy funerals or mourning. Get on with your lives. Have fun with this – I know you will!' So anyhow, Paige, her attorney sent this to me after he called to tell me of her passing."

"Wow. That note sounds just like her. I can't believe she actually had a will. She was never one for 'the paperwork,' as she called it."

"Well, she did. And you're never going to believe this ... she left us the Snapdragon Inn!"

"She what?!"

"She left us the inn! Me and you!"

"The whole inn? She left us the Snapdragon?"

Glo stood up and did a little happy dance around the room, waving the envelope in the air. I sat there staring at her in disbelief. Finally, she sat down and opened the envelope.

"She has a letter in here for us. I waited to open it until we were together. Ready for me to read it now?"

"Yes, please," I whispered. Shockwaves were running through me.

Glo reached into the manila envelope and brought out a letter. She took a sip of tea and put on her reading glasses. She unfolded the paper and began to read.

My dearest granddaughter, Gloria and great-

granddaughter, Paige,

If you're reading this, it's because I'm gone. I want you both to be happy, so none of that prolonged grieving stuff. Bye, bye GeeGee! It's been great! Seriously. I will haunt you if you disobey. I'll give you one hour of moping about then get on with it. Don't worry about me, I'm in a much better place. You both mean the world to me, and I'll miss you dearly, but I'm taking a piece of you with me in my heart.

"Leave it to GeeGee," I laughed. "She's passed away, but she'll miss us."

Glo chuckled and looked up at the ceiling. "We miss you too, GeeGee."

Everything I own and everything I value is part of the Snapdragon Inn. The home, the glorious property, and all my earthly belongings I am giving to the two of you. I can't think of a better pair to carry on my legacy.

Gloria, I know you. You're wondering why I haven't left this to Paige's mother, your sister Julie. Well, to be honest, she has no sense of adventure or enthusiasm for life. She'd probably turn the inn into a Hilton and focus on making a profit. Don't worry about her, I left her a nice chunk of money and she'll go invest it wisely or do some other sensible thing. You and Paige, on the other hand, are impulsive and curious and prone to being the opposite of boring, practical, and sensible.

"Hey, GeeGee!" I laughed. "Not sure that's the compliment you intended it to be."

Glo nodded. "But it's clear she meant we were fun-loving and carefree, just like she was."

Snapdragon has everything in it that you need to have a full, exciting life together. Every room is fully decorated, the kitchen and bathrooms are stocked with everything you need. The house is move-in ready, and I've left you sufficient funds to run the inn. I made sure of that before I left this world.

I'm putting the two of you in charge of the secret library. It's priceless, and I wouldn't entrust it to anyone else. Choose wisely, and I hope you have the time of your lives!

"Library? Choose wisely? What is she talking about?"

"Maybe it's that locked room in the basement she never let us go into?" Glo said. "If it's priceless, perhaps she had a collection she was keeping safe. And she must mean choose wisely which books to read, or maybe which to sell?"

"Wow! That's crazy. She said she gave my mom – how did she phrase it?"

"A nice chunk of money," said Glo.

"Right. Maybe she does have a valuable book collection hidden down there?"

Glo shrugged her shoulders. "And here we thought we knew everything about her."

I have assigned a caregiver to keep the inn running smoothly until you arrive. My lawyer is handling the scheduling and payments. He'll transfer everything over to you when you've arrived in Cascade Valley. What are you waiting for? Pack up your bags and get moving, girls!

I love you both. Happy travels!

GeeGee
XOXO

"Well?" Glo looked at me, then she waved her arms dramatically around my small apartment still filled with boxes from my move. "You ready to leave all this?"

"That would be insane ... I'd have to let my lease expire. I'd have to quit my job!"

"So? You hate this apartment, and you hate your job!"

"I don't know. That would be so impulsive."

"That's what makes it wonderful, Paige!"

"What if I don't get another job?"

She held up one finger. "First, you know you could get another job, if you wanted to." She dramatically held up a second finger. "Second, you have plenty of money in your rainy-day account as a bridge."

She was right. I'd opened the account soon after I got married to save for the day that Spencer and I called it quits. I had no idea it would turn out to be so many years' worth of savings.

"Besides, use your noggin girl. You'll have a job." Glo tapped herself in the temple.

"Huh?"

"Running the inn!"

"I don't know anything about running an inn!"

"It's a regular house with a few rented rooms. You've managed an entire office for years. I think we'll be able to figure it out. How hard could it be?"

"You're starting to make sense." I shook my head. I couldn't believe I was actually considering this. "What about you, Glo?"

"You know I can write anywhere there's a computer and internet. So, I'll just take my work with me. And I'll rent out my house. We can sell or give away what we don't want to take with us. You can sell your car and we'll take the truck and a U-Haul. Unless you want to keep your car and drive separately. But honestly, your rig would be worthless on those mountain passes."

"It sounds like you've already planned all this!"

"How much planning does it take? We have a house. We pack up. We go."

"But ... my mom will go crazy if we just pack up and leave!"

"Because she's *boring, practical, and sensible.*" Glo laughed, quoting GeeGee. "Come on, Paige! If there's any time in your life to do this, it's right now. You're a free woman! Can you think of a better way to get a fresh start?"

2

I shut the U-Haul door with a satisfying snap and dusted my hands off on my jeans. I turned around, looked at my apartment building and gave it a salute. Out with the old, in with the new.

It had been a whirlwind couple of weeks since the Big Decision. Selling my car and our furniture, sorting, packing, and cleaning. Quitting my job had been the easy part. Then the grand finale – telling my mother what we were doing. GeeGee always said, "Julie is the serious one, Glo is the fun one." True to form, my mother thought we were out of our minds, but honestly, she was so distracted planning the investment of her inheritance that she basically sent us off with a wave, wishing us luck.

~ ~ ~

I hopped up into my aunt's truck. I moved aside the four full bags of road snacks and drinks. "All set. Let's hit the road!"

"Can you take a picture of our route map? We'll lose service going through the mountain pass, and I don't want to get lost."

"Got it." I immediately did as Glo suggested. We'd learned our lesson the hard way when we'd been halfway to our destination last summer and lost service. We ended up going an hour out of our way.

Since my mother did the driving when I was a kid, and then Spencer insisted on driving when I'd gone with him to visit GeeGee, I had no idea how to get there. I'd always been busy sightseeing and snacking. Glo was such an unobservant driver that she never remembered the route from one trip to the next, she drove absent-mindedly, following the voice on her GPS without question.

Sure enough, when we hit the pass, we lost service. When I looked at my photos, I realized I had cut off one step. Of course, it was the one I needed right now.

"I'm pretty sure you get on US 50," I said.

"Pretty sure that doesn't give me much confidence in my navigator," Glo said as she took the turn.

As we drove higher into the mountain pass, the road narrowed.

"This is barely wide enough for two cars, I hope a big truck doesn't come around the—"

My eyes nearly popped out of my head when an enormous hay truck came whipping around the corner forcing us to the edge of the road. This would have been a challenge on any day but hauling a trailer behind us made it terrifying.

I turned my head and made the mistake of glancing out the window. My stomach lurched as I looked down, down, down over a thousand feet of cliffside. Although we had slowed to a crawl, all I could think was *if a tire blows right now, we're toast.*

I sat perfectly still in the passenger seat and held my breath, afraid any movement might distract Glo. She was a great driver, and I trusted her big, heavy truck, but this winding mountain road was scary enough without having to pass a truck on a hairpin curve with no guardrail – while pulling a U-Haul filled with all our earthly possessions.

As we squeezed by the hay truck I sucked in my stomach and pressed myself back against the seat, instinctively making myself smaller — that would certainly help. As if in slow motion the hay truck passed us and then disappeared in my side-view mirror. Glo puffed out a breath and her whole body visibly deflated.

"It doesn't build much confidence when my driver's knuckles are white and she's wiping her sweaty palms on her jeans and hyperventilating," I teased.

"Hey, do you want to drive?" she asked.

"No! Thanks anyway, but I kind of like living. Were you able to see any of the scenery?"

"Are you freakin' kidding me?" Glo squealed. "I was kind of busy here, driving a truck and pulling a U-Haul on the road from crazyville. I couldn't take my eyes off the road. It's like what they say about race car drivers, you know?"

"No, what do that say?" I asked.

"They're taught to keep their eyes on where they want to go, not where they don't. In other words, don't look at the wall." Glo gripped the steering wheel with both hands as she kept her eyes forward. "In this case: the cliff! There's no way I was looking anywhere but in front of me!"

I shivered at the thought. "The valley was gorgeous though. I saw an alpine lake way down below us. It was a vibrant sapphire blue! I was afraid to take a picture though, I didn't want to distract you."

"Yeah, that's good. Because passengers taking photos always leads to me erratically swerving off a cliff."

"Hah!" I'd been taking a sip of water when she said that and was laughing so hard I spit water all over the dash in front of me. I wiped up the water and resisted opening another bag of popcorn. I didn't want to make her erratically swerve off the cliff by opening a crinkly bag.

Happily, the stretch in front of us looked relatively benign. Only a few more hairpin turns with less gruesome cliffs and a few barely reassuring two-foot-high guard rails. Once we made it off the treacherous mountain road it was basically a straight shot to Cascade Valley. We chatted, snacked, and enjoyed the beauty of the scenery.

~ ~ ~

When we pulled up to the Snapdragon Inn, I was flooded with memories of my last visit here just a few months ago, mixed with many from my childhood. I'd spent plenty of vacation days here in this home. It felt familiar, and it embraced me with the warmth of my carefree childhood summers.

The home was a spectacular example of a cozy lakeside country inn. Painted white with deep green shutters, it boasted a porch that lined the entire front of the building. Hanging baskets bursting with colorful flowers decorated the posts, and more flowers lined the picket fence out front. There were two porch swings with bright green striped pillows. There had always been porch swings here, and GeeGee would let me sit outside and swing while I enjoyed a popsicle or a slice of watermelon.

The huge round gazebo at the far end of the porch was host to a dinner table with plenty of room for almost a dozen people to enjoy an outdoor meal.

I knew that around the back side of the house

was a vast green lawn leading down to the lake. Each of the eight bedrooms had a personal deck looking out over the view, with comfy seating and a small table for private time and reflection.

The backyard always had Adirondack chairs for the guests' enjoyment. These were placed under a willow tree to provide shade from the summer sun. After dark, the yard came alive with twinkle lights and a crackling fire pit where we'd make s'mores or roast hot dogs.

The dock off the yard always had several canoes and a few paddle boards at this time of year. I'd learned to row and swim in this lake.

"GeeGee's house is magnificent, isn't it? A breathtaking beauty." I sighed.

"Honey, it's our house now." Glo put her arm around me, and we both stood and stared at our fresh start.

"Want to go inside and poke around before we unpack?" asked Glo.

"Sure! It'll be nice to stretch our legs and get the lay of the land."

The front door opened just as we stepped onto the deck and an older man with fashionably styled white hair and a closely trimmed beard stepped outside. He looked relaxed in a plaid flannel shirt, but his jeans were obviously new and even boasted a crease from being ironed.

"Gloria and Paige, I would assume?" He smiled and reached out a hand. "I'm Theodore Van Lambert, but you can call me Theo. Clara's instructions were for me to watch over the place until you arrived."

It always sounded funny to me when someone called my great-grandmother by her given name. She was always GeeGee to everyone in the family and to all the guests of her inn, as well.

"Everything's in order here, so I'm heading out. We don't have any guests at the present time. All reservations were canceled after Clara left us. It will be up to you when to fill up the rooms again, of course. Here're my numbers; call or text me if you ladies need anything."

Theo handed us each a card with his information, then walked off toward the garage. We stepped in through the front door that he'd left open for us.

~ ~ ~

"Ahhhh." We both let out a sigh of pleasure. This home had looked exactly the same ever since I was a little girl. It was the closest thing to a hug that a building could provide. The warm wooden ceiling and bronze-colored walls were marvelous. At night they reflected back the light from twin chandeliers designed to look like dozens of lit candles. The fireplace that soared to the ceiling was created from rocks found on the property. Similar rocks were used to create two massive columns that set the dining area off from the living room. An abundance of live plants, tapestries, and artwork, plus the comfy brown leather furniture gave the room a homey lived-in feeling. The not-a-bear rug in front of the fireplace made me smile. GeeGee was adamant about telling everyone who entered that it wasn't from a real bear. I often wondered why she kept it if she were so concerned what people would think. It did fit the décor, so perhaps that was the simple reason.

The two of us stood inside the entry absorbing the beauty. I was mesmerized and had goosebumps thinking that this glorious place was now where we would call home.

3

I was so enthralled with the main room I hadn't even realized Glo had moved to the kitchen. I joined her there, marveling at the bright, open space that somehow balanced the soothing mood of the living room. Unlike some small inns, this home was built for the purpose, so there was no need to struggle to transform a personal home into an inn. This area was surprisingly large and housed both the kitchen and eating nook with a lovely archway between them. The nook looked out over the back yard and the lake through two sets of double doors. These would be opened on warm, sunny days – and luckily in Colorado there were plenty of those. The long wooden table always featured a unique centerpiece, often made from the flowers found in the yard. There was no centerpiece today, but I made a note to remedy that. I wanted to uphold those lovely traditions.

The archway that divided the kitchen from the nook was hung with ivy that softened its appearance to make it appear more as an invitation than a separation. The kitchen itself was designed as a workspace to create meals for large groups but decorated with a small-town country charm. The white painted cabinets were set off by swirly patterned granite and highlighted by a group of hanging lamps that looked like crystal globes. My favorite place in the kitchen was a booth set off to the side. It was tucked on the edge of the room to provide the owners some privacy away from the guests. It was close enough that I'd sit there with a book or my drawing kit while GeeGee cooked a meal or baked bread or cookies.

"Want some tea or coffee?" Glo asked. "There's a Keurig here. There are even refillable pods. You know GeeGee and her commitment to sustainability."

"Think I'll go for coffee. I'm going to need a dose of energy to get that U-Haul unpacked."

"Ugh, yeah. Good times ahead. Let's pick our bedrooms first, so we know where to move the boxes," Glo suggested.

Coffee mugs in hand we slowly walked through the house and up the stairs. The second floor featured eight bedrooms, each with its own ensuite bathroom. The first room at the top of the stairs had been GeeGee's. It still smelled like her rose-scented perfume.

"Oh, my eyes!" laughed Glo as she covered both eyes with her hand. "This room is chintz overload! It's like a fabric shop exploded in here."

"She was the queen of chintz, that's for sure. As if the bedspread, drapes, and sofa weren't enough! When she decided to wallpaper in chintz, I stopped coming up here. The chaos of floral patterns muddled my brain."

"So, I'm guessing you don't want this room, Paige? It's the biggest bedroom. I thought I'd have to fight you for it."

"You're not really going to use this room, are you?"

"Yeah. I think I am." She sniffed.

The seriousness of her voice took me by surprise. I looked over at her and realized her eyes were wet with tears. She hastily wiped them away and I could tell she didn't want me to bring it up.

"It makes me feel close to her, so yeah. I call dibs on the chintz palace."

"You got it," I said.

We wandered down the hallway peeking in every room. The bedrooms were a feast for the eyes. Every single guest room was decorated differently, and they often changed. My great-grandmother said she loved the novelty of having unique rooms to suit the different personalities of her guests. The rooms were not just different, some of them looked like they came from a totally different home – some from a different country.

"I've always loved the Zen peacefulness of the Japanese garden room," I said.

"The simplicity of it makes me itch," said Glo, scratching her arms. "Way too much empty space for my liking."

I opened the next door. "Oh, wow! This room is spectacular! I wonder when she did this?"

Glo squeezed past me and stepped into the room. "Holy confetti! This is something else."

"If the room were totally empty of furniture, but had these gorgeous walls, I'd still want to live in this space!" I walked over to the side and gently slid my hand over the painted wall. "It's almost 3D. The branches feel like wood."

"This has been hand-painted. It must have taken a year!"

We both stood in the center of the room and slowly turned circles to take it all in. Two of the walls were covered floor to ceiling with the textured wall painting. The background was a pale blue and white, the colors of the sky on a summer day. The gradient colors were overlayed with many golden-brown branches of a cherry tree in bloom. Here and there were tiny birds and butterflies. It was wonderfully beautiful. If the walls weren't enough to mesmerize me, the furniture was delicate but cozy, matching the darkest blue colors from the painted walls. In addition to the bed there was a seating area with two overstuffed chairs and a table, the base of which was a cherry tree branch.

"Oh, this is definitely my room!" I hugged myself. "Are you okay with that?"

"Of course I am." She smirked at me. "How could this possibly compare with chintz town?"

Once we laid stake to our rooms, we peeked in all the others just to see what they looked like. It was a potpourri of fun and adventure and made me even more excited about living here.

"Hey Glo, before we unpack, can we go look in the library downstairs? GeeGee never let me in there and I'm dying of curiosity!"

"Oooh, yeah. Let's do. I understand her not letting us in there as kids, but come on, at some point she should have let us in there. I can't imagine why she kept it so hush-hush."

Glo and I took the stairs all the way down to the basement, but we found the door locked up tight. We texted Theo, but he said he was never given a key. I called a local locksmith and he said he'd be out the next morning. There were no other reasons to delay unloading the truck, so we grabbed another cup of coffee and finally got to the task.

4

Waking up in my pretty new room filled with cherry tree blossoms gave me a wave of happiness and excitement. I spotted more tiny birds and butterflies hiding among the branches, and to my delight a few caterpillars, as well. This was the first day of my new life, and I planned to make the most of it. I made a promise to myself not to look backwards, but to stay forward thinking. Forward was easy. Forward was bright. Forward was new. I would keep my eyes there, and not look back.

I showered in my lovely pink and blue bathroom, then dressed in my ridiculously large closet filled with built-in shelves and drawers. If I shopped for a year I'd never fill all these spaces. I found that I enjoyed the empty spaces. They felt fresh, like my life.

"Morning, Glo! Coffee smells wonderful."

"Look! I made breakfast, too!" She proudly pointed with both hands.

I glanced at the pans on the stove and the plates on the counter. Overcooked eggs beaten to a pulp, undercooked bacon, and burnt toast. Or were those English muffins? It was hard to tell. I loved my aunt, but I did not love her cooking. She looked so pleased to have breakfast ready that I choked it down with a grin.

The sound of a gong filled the kitchen and we both laughed at GeeGee's ridiculous doorbell sound.

"I'll get it," I said, glad to walk away from my half-eaten breakfast.

"I'm sure it's the locksmith," she said, following me. I had a feeling she didn't want the breakfast, either.

"I've never seen anything like this," said the locksmith. He took a step back and scratched his head. He'd been at it for twenty minutes and still hadn't opened the door. "It doesn't make sense. This takes a skeleton key. It should be a simple task. People can do it with a couple of Allen wrenches. I've even done it with a pair of paperclips."

"So, what do we do now?" Glo asked.

"Best thing is to contact a carpenter. Since the hinges are inside, he'll have to drill the lock. It'll destroy the lock and damage your door, though."

"We don't have much choice. We want to get into the room, so we'll have to do it," I said. "Why call a contractor, though? Can't we just take a drill to it ourselves?"

"It's not exactly an easy process, especially hard if you've never done it before. You need to drill the lock at the shear line so that it separates the driver pins and key pins that hold the mechanism in place. Then you have to rotate the plug and align it to unlock the door."

"Shear line? Driver pins? Align the plugs?" asked Glo.

"No, it's separate the pins and then rotate the plugs," I corrected her.

"And what the heck are pins and plugs Miss Home Improvement Paige the Toolman?" Glo and the locksmith both laughed.

"Fine," I huffed. "We'll call a contractor."

After the locksmith left, we looked up a couple of

local contractors, but any openings were days away. We texted Theo but hadn't heard back from him yet.

We decided to start the day by sorting out the kitchen. There were plenty of dishes and dry goods, but the organization was an absolute mess.

"How in the world did she work in this disaster?" Glo mumbled. "You'd spend half your time searching for things!" She was emptying out a cabinet. She pulled out an odd assortment of dishes, pots, cleaning supplies, and canned goods. She started to laugh and held up a hundred-piece puzzle in one hand and a shoeshine kit in the other.

"Now this makes perfect sense." She was snorting. "Make dinner, clean up, shine your shoes and do a puzzle."

I held up a few treasures from the cabinet I was working on. "And here you go. In case you need a spare pair of socks, a stack of plastic containers – no lids – and printer ink."

"It's like a treasure hunt! It's good for us to sort through all this anyhow."

"True," I agreed. "Then we'll know what we've got. Let me find some paper and a pen and we'll start a list of things we need."

I began to sort through the typical drawers most people would use for things like pens and scratch paper, then groaned. "You know what's in her junk drawers? Talcum powder, coffee creamer, clothespins, and aha! The soup bowls!"

"Where's the very last place you'd look for a pen and paper? Try that first," snickered Glo.

"Probably the bathroom," I joked. "I'll just make a list on my phone."

I opened another cabinet and groaned at the stack of boxes and plastic containers jammed into every inch. They were filled with random stuff. I took them to the table and dumped them out.

"Have you found any trash bags? Lots of this is garbage."

Glo handed me a bag and I started sorting the hodgepodge of items.

"Holy Toledo! Glo, look at this!" I stood up and did a little dance around the kitchen. I shimmied over to her, then held up a very old-looking skeleton key.

~ ~ ~

"I feel like we should have a drum roll or a trumpet fanfare—"

"—or fireworks!" laughed Glo. "At least a countdown. Five ... four ... three ... two ... one! – blastoff!"

I turned the key and heard the click as it unlocked. "Houston, we have liftoff."

I twisted the knob and pushed the door open. There was a set of stairs to the basement. At the bottom of the stairs was another door. We opened it. Impossibly, there was another set of stairs. At the bottom of those stairs was yet another door. It required a skeleton key to open. I stared at the key in my hand. "You better work," I told the key.

The key worked smoothly, and I opened the door.

Our jaws dropped and neither of us spoke. You could have heard a cotton ball drop.

Finally, Glo broke the silence. "Holy macaroni! This is insane!"

"How could she have kept this secret our whole lives?" I wondered.

"WHY did she keep this secret?" Glo added.

"This room is the size of the entire house! It's enormous. Ginormous!" I whistled.

"This secret space is underneath the inn! How is it two stories high? Is that even structurally sound? This is bizarre."

The room was indeed two levels high, connected by a brass spiral staircase. In the front area, where we were glued to the spot, was a large seating area with eight cozy floral patterned armchairs. A beautiful wooden coffee table sat in the middle. There was an antique globe on a brass stand, and a stone fireplace like the one upstairs. This one had an intricately carved wood mantle and a stone hearth. A large statue of a woman holding a book was centered on the mantle.

"Look at all these books!" exclaimed Glo, spinning in a circle.

"This is the library GeeGee referred to in her will! Remember? She said she's putting us in charge. That it's priceless!"

"I am beyond confused, Paige. How is this even possible? GeeGee was just a sweet little innkeeper. She was the lady who baked us cookies and homemade stew. And she was hiding all this right under our feet?!"

"There must be *thousands* of books here." My eyes were darting around the room. I could hardly believe what I was seeing.

Both levels of the room were covered from end-to-end with bookshelves that were lined with books. We were still rooted to the spot, too awestruck to move.

"Meowzer!"

A gorgeous chocolate point Siamese cat came out from behind a bookcase.

"Oh, my God! It's a cat!" said Glo. "How did a cat get down here?"

"Glo. Did that cat say 'meowzer'?"

"Paige, Siamese are known for their distinctive voices. Remember Uncle Syd's Siamese? Syd used to say that they were notorious for their distinctive vocal antics."

The cat climbed up onto one of the chair backs and stared at us with big blue eyes. Then he cleared his throat.

I looked at Glo and raised my eyebrows. "And what was that?"

"Probably just a cat noise. Like coughing up a hairball or something."

"Glo. That didn't sound very cat-like. Do Siamese cough like humans, too? That sounded more like Syd than his cat."

"Well, like I said, Siamese express their feelings with many different sounds, and—"

"If you chickens are done clucking?" the cat said in an extremely uncatlike voice. Then he cleared his throat again.

"Gooood morning! Ladies and ... umm ... gentleladies! If I may have your attention. I give you the star of the show, the amazing, the wonderful, the host to all your dreams and wishes – okay, not so much wishes, really, but—

"Where was I before I was interrupted?" He scowled at us, as if we'd been the ones to interrupt, then continued. "Oh yeah. The host to all your dreams and the guide to your future adventures ... introducing ... Me!" The cat took a dramatic bow and fell off the chair, landing in a laughing heap on the floor. Laughing a man's laugh. More like my uncle Syd than his Siamese cat.

"Are you hearing what I'm hearing?" I asked Glo

out of the side of my mouth.

"The cat is talking," said Glo out of the side of her mouth.

"Yeah. He is," said the cat out of the side of his furry little mouth.

We stared at the cat.

He stared back at us with his keen blue eyes.

5

"Why the confusion?" The sleek Siamese jumped back up on the chair and tilted his head at us. "Pfffft. It's like you've never heard a talking cat before."

We continued to stare at him.

"Cat got your tongue?" He guffawed and snorted.

"Are you really a talking cat?" I asked as I walked a circle around the chair inspecting the area.

"Whatcha' lookin' for?" the cat said.

"I am looking for a hidden person, or a tape recorder – or something to explain how that voice appears to be coming out of your mouth."

"Uh, Paige," said Glo. "I think the voice *is* coming out of his mouth. I think it's a talking cat."

"You think?" gasped the cat. "You THINK! Honey, scoot yourself on over here and pay verrry close attention. Do you understand the words that are coming out of my mouth?" Then he guffawed again at his parody of Chris Tucker's voice and the famous line from the movie *Rush Hour*.

"Let's say you really are talking—"

"Yeah. Let's say that," said the cat, flicking a whisker.

"How is it possible?" I asked.

"Uhm. You're talking. How is that possible?"

I decided to skip to the next question. "Were you GeeGee's cat?"

"It's complicated. You could say I come with the library. I suppose that would make me your cat now, in a manner of speaking, or perhaps you're my people." He chuckled. "I mean, someone must feed me since

I'm unable to drive myself to the grocery store. As you might imagine. My cat door permits me to do my unmentionable business outside, and Theo has filled in with cat chow, but now it's up to you two."

"What's your name?" asked Glo.

I turned to her. "Are you just skipping over the logical details and jumping right into hey, there talking cat, what's your name?"

"At least one of you has some manners," mumbled the cat. "Allow me to introduce myself. The name's Frank."

I burst out laughing. Glo gave me the side eye and whispered, "Shh."

"Oh, and I suppose Paige is the name of the year?" He lifted his chin. "Frank would be short for Franklin. The name of one of our great presidents. Plus, frank is also a tasty meat dish and the concept of sincerity and honesty. And what about you, Miss Paige, the flat piece of paper?"

"How do you know who I am?" I skipped right over his mockery of my name, feeling badly that I laughed at his. It was just ridiculously absurd that this sleek, gorgeous cat could talk. And that his name was Frank.

"My dear girl, GeeGee told me about the two of you before she left us. Obviously, since you were named in the will, I would need to be aware of your arrival."

"It's very nice to meet you, Frank." Glo went over to him and shook his little paw. I rolled my eyes but followed suit. His paw was soft and silky, but his handshake was firm.

"My grandmother never told us about you or this library," said Glo. "And we've both been to the inn many, many times. Do you know why she kept it a secret?"

"Yep."

"Can you tell us?"

"Nope."

"Why not?" I asked.

"Are you always so incessantly curious?" Frank jumped down off the chair and walked in a circle around me.

I shrugged my shoulders. "I suppose."

Glo laughed. "Yes, she most certainly is." She leaned closer to the cat and whispered, "It can be a touch annoying sometimes."

The cat chuckled. "It will serve her well."

I closed my eyes and shook my head. I had a million questions on the tip of my tongue but chose to stay quiet after that comment.

"Would you ladies like a tour?" Frank asked.

"Yes, please!" we both answered.

Frank walked back and forth in front of the many bookshelves. "These here are the books. There's more upstairs." He tilted his head back and his eyes wobbled back and forth around the room, as if pointing to the many shelves. Then he walked over to the seating area. "This here is the meeting space for the book club. End of tour. Thank you very much for your attention. Tips accepted."

Frank jumped back up on one of the armchairs and proceeded to groom his front paw.

"Is this the stage of the tour where we can ask questions?"

"And there she is again with the questions."

He looked at Glo and they nodded at each other. Great. They'd already formed an alliance.

"Sure, honey. Ask away."

I paused. I hadn't really expected him to say yes, and wasn't sure what to ask first, or how to ask it. "Umm. Uh. How many books are down here?"

"Don't know. Never counted 'em. Next."

"Why are they here?"

"Ahh. Good question." He looked straight at me and twitched his tail.

"Um, why are they here?"

"Heard ya. Can't tell ya."

"Okay, then. You mentioned a book club?"

"Ding! Ding! Ding! The winning question. Now that one I can answer. The owner of the library —or in your case, owners – are required to host a book club of exactly eight members to begin with."

"Really? I never saw GeeGee host a book club."

"Indeed. You never saw her."

"Because ..."

"Because she only hosted the group when you were not visiting. Because it was—"

He leaned toward me and cocked his head expectantly.

"Because it was secret!" shouted Glo.

"Excellent! You go to the head of the class, Gloria," said Frank.

"Oh, do you mind calling me Glo?"

"You got it. Glo it is. Suits you."

"Thanks." She smiled at the cat. My aunt was taking to this very strange situation as if it were all perfectly normal. I wasn't really surprised. Glo was like that.

"I don't understand," I started. "What—"

"Of course you don't understand. I haven't explained it yet. You are to collect six more willing participants. The two of you being seven and eight. Then gather here." He jerked his head toward the seating area. "Once the group does their chatting, get to know you stuff, then the group selects a mystery to read."

"Oh, where is the mystery book section?" I asked.

"They are allll the mystery book section." Frank drew out the word *all* with a trill of his tongue.

"All the books are mysteries?"

"They are. Cozy mysteries to be precise. We don't do graphic violence, swearing, or sex around here. Well, not in the books anyway." He chuckled. "Plenty of intrigue and suspense. Twists and turns. And the sleuths are amateurs. Obviously." He looked us up and down. "So, what was I saying? Oh, yeah, the group agrees on a book for the club and there you have it!"

"That sounds fun!" said Glo. "And it will be a great way to get to know the people in our community."

"I agree! It sounds great." I glanced around the room "Wow, look at that beautiful antique typewriter." I walked over to the display case next to the fireplace. An antique Underwood sat in the glass case. Several ancient looking books, two carved wooden vases, and several ornate paperweights completed the display. A gold plaque read, *The Mystery Ends Here.*

"Do not be touching that," Frank said.

"It looks like an antique," Glo pointed out.

Frank nodded. "Rare and exceptional."

"The statue on the fireplace, is that an antique also?" I took a closer look. It appeared to be bronze, and it also had a gold plaque. This one read, *The Magical Mystery Book Club.*

"That's the name of it," said Frank.

"The name of the statue?"

"Nope. The name of your fancy-schmancy new club."

"So why do we have to have eight members?" I asked. "Because there are eight chairs?"

"Ah, brilliant deduction!" He puffed his two hands together in what I assumed was applause. "But no. Not it. Go take a closer peek at a shelf. But don't remove any books until the entire club is gathered."

Glo and I moved closer to a bookshelf.

"Ah!" She pointed but didn't touch. "Each title has

eight copies tied together with twine!"

"You, my dear are smart as a whip. You might even be able to keep up with yours truly."

"Where do we find people for the club?" Glo asked. "We don't know anyone yet."

"GeeGee would post a notice on the bulletin board at the grocery store in town when there was an opening. A great place to purchase cat food, tuna, shrimp, and salmon, by the way. In case you were wondering what I most enjoy for meals."

"We have to pick up groceries, and we need to return the U-Haul. I guess we'll post a notice while we're there."

"Jolly good decision; press on my dears," said Frank in a very poorly done English accent.

6

We walked quietly up the stairs, then I closed the door and locked it. I went dazedly into the kitchen, found a purple lanyard that I'd seen in one of the random boxes, and clipped the key to it. I hung it over a hook near the door. Then I turned around and planted myself on the sofa, my arms limp at my sides.

Glo sat on the chair across from me, her brows knit, an incredulous look on her face.

"What the heck?" I exhaled the words.

She threw up her hands and shrugged her shoulders. Then she let out a bark of laughter. Her laugh was so free and full of joy that I couldn't help joining her. Soon we were both holding our guts and wiping tears from our eyes.

I looked up at the ceiling. "GeeGee, you sure got us good!"

"Can you believe it?" Glo asked.

A fluttery feeling of excitement tingled through my body. "I think this is the absolute coolest thing that's ever happened to me."

"Pffft. It's like you've never heard a talking cat before." She mimicked Frank's deep voice, which got us both howling in laughter again.

"Okay. Stop, stop," I gasped. "We're really doing this, right? Start a book club with a bunch of strangers and begin a friendship with a cat-man?"

"A cat-man?" Glo began to giggle but put her hand over her mouth. "You don't think he can hear us up here, do you?"

"Geeze, I hope not. He did say he was going

to take a nap." I pulled out my phone. "Let's do it! New beginnings, right? Let's write up a book club announcement. When do we want to start this thing?"

"How about Saturday?" Glo suggested. "In case people work, it might be better than a weekday."

"Sounds good. We should also pick an opening date for guests and post that as well. It'll take money to keep the house going, so we should do that sooner rather than later."

"I suppose, but the house is pretty much ready," Glo pointed out. "GeeGee left us plenty of cash. I'm sure she knew what it took to pay the bills and wanted to give us time to get settled. How about we give ourselves a week or two to find our footing?"

"Makes sense." I got up and retrieved the paper and pen that I'd finally found in the kitchen. "So ... the book club. How about noon, and make it a potluck so everyone can get to know one another?"

"I like that idea. Let's make those tear-off tabs on the bottom. We'll have them text ahead, so we don't go over the eight-person limit."

I sat and wrote out the poster while Glo fiddled with her Instagram account. When I finished, I showed her the result.

"Very nice! You're hired!"

"What am I hired for?" I asked.

"Uhh. Making book club posters, I guess?"

~ ~ ~

We returned the U-Haul first, and I was glad to be rid of it. Just looking at it made me think of that ridiculous mountain road and those terrifying hairpin turns. I was neither an adrenaline junkie nor a race car driver. I'd take a nice safe, ground-level road, thank you very much.

The town of Cascade Valley was charming and inviting. It was so safe here that GeeGee would let my friends and me wander into town for ice cream all on our own. It was nice to be back.

There was only one grocery store in town, so the community bulletin board was easy to find. Unlike many I'd seen, this one was neat and orderly. None of those rude people pinning their own notices over the top of others. These were all lined up like little soldiers. I added ours to the ranks.

"Hey, Glo. I know we're going to spend a fortune on groceries, but I'll be too tired to cook anything when we get home. Want to go somewhere and eat first? Then we can shop."

"A woman after my own heart," said Glo. "What are you in the mood for?"

"I don't know. What's here?"

We drove around the block and landed at a friendly looking Mexican restaurant. We filled up on chips and salsa then split an order of fajitas. We even splurged on margaritas. The conversation, of course, was dominated by the library and Frank.

"I just can't wrap my head around the fact that GeeGee kept this enormous secret our entire lives. Why wouldn't she share it with us?" I grabbed another chip and loaded it up with salsa.

Glo suddenly looked sad. "I wish she was still here so we could ask her."

"Me too, Aunt Glo."

She shook her body, as if ridding herself of the grieving emotions. "Shall we go get all Frank's food at the market?"

I laughed at that. "I have a feeling that cat is

going to spice up our lives."

We returned to the market, filled a cart with food for us and the cat, then we headed home.

~ ~ ~

"Who's that?"

Glo pulled her truck into the garage. "Where?"

"There's a little white-haired lady sitting on our porch swing."

"Haven't a clue."

"Let's find out before we unload the groceries." I suggested. "Maybe she's a potential guest?"

We walked toward the front door, both of us assessing the woman.

"Whoa. She's tiny! She looks like she's about a hundred years old," Glo said.

We stepped up on the porch.

"Not a hundred yet!" She pointed to her hearing aids. "Bionic ears. Can hear everything." She smiled a youthful smile filled with clean, white teeth. She pointed to them, then tapped the shiny enamel. "Bionic teeth too." She bounced up off the swing with more energy than I had on most days.

"Zelda Finkelstein. Octogenarian, and proud of it! Especially when you consider the alternative. Just had a birthday. Now I'm the ripe young age of eighty. That means I've tossed all my filters. All of 'em!" She used both hands as finger guns and aimed them at us. "Bang. Bang. Watch out." She holstered her guns, then thrust her hand out toward me.

"Nice to meet you," I reached down and shook her remarkably teeny hand. "Paige Erickson."

"I thought it was Paige Turner. You certainly are one. A page turner. Sure you've heard that one before." She snickered. "Lovely young woman, you are."

"Umm. I recovered my maiden name, so it's Erickson now."

"'Spose that's for the best. Leave the old ball and chain behind, no reason to keep a name you don't want. And you must be Gloria?" She turned to my aunt with her miniscule hand extended.

Glo looked down into the woman's bright eyes. "Yes, I'm Gloria. But you can call me Glo."

Zelda giggled. Yep, she giggled. "Glow! Oh, my gosh! I just love that. Glow! Maybe I should be ... Zell. Yep, let's do that." She turned and held a hand out to me again.

"Hello, I'm Zell Finkelstein." Then she giggled again and repeated the action to Glo.

Glo laughed, her eyes twinkling. "Well, it's awful nice to meet you Zell Finkelstein."

"Just Zell, honey. I don't have time for the whole thing."

"How can we help you?" I asked.

"I'm here about the book club." She walked to the front door and tried to open it, but it was locked.

"Whatcha' locking your door for? This ain't no New York City, you know. Folks don't go into homes where they don't belong."

We gaped at her.

"Well, who's got the key? Let's get this show on the road." She clapped her hands.

I pulled out my key chain and unlocked the door. We followed Zell into the house. She went directly to the kitchen and started opening and closing cabinets.

She let out a hoot. "You girls are already reorganizing things, huh? GeeGee never had time for that. Said as long as she knew where things were, it was fine and dandy. Problem was, she never knew where things were. It was always an Easter egg hunt. So, where's the tea fixens'?"

Glo opened a cabinet and began to pull down the tea bags and sugar, but Zell batted her hand away.

"Just because I'm old doesn't mean I can't make a cup of tea, young lady. Just point me to your footstool and I'll whip us up a little snack."

Glo put her hand over her mouth to control her giggles. I wasn't quick enough, and a laugh escaped me.

"Oh, I'm sorry," I said, tamping down my laughter.

"Sorry? Sorry for what? Laughter?! You go right on laughing at my antics. Laughing is a good thing. And you know what? I tell my kids and grandkids and great-grands that if I get senile they should go right ahead and laugh the heck out of me. Life is better with a sense of humor, don't you think?" She smiled, showing off her brilliant white bionic teeth and a darling set of dimples.

Glo and I sat at the kitchen booth and watched Zell putter around the kitchen. She refused to let us tell her where things were. She said it was too much fun figuring it out.

Finally, we had tea, crackers, cheese, and a can of sardines in front of us.

"Oh!" I stood up. "We have groceries in the car. We better bring them in."

"I'll help!" She jumped right over to the door that led to the garage, opened it, stepped out, and was lugging in the first bag almost before we got to the truck.

I glanced at Glo and we both attempted to control our shock at this wild little spitfire.

"You gals gettin' the bags or not?" Zell said over her shoulder as she took the first bag inside.

As Glo and I were putting things away, Zell finally sat down and made herself a cup of tea. She opened the sardines, putting a piece on top of a cracker with cheese and took a dainty bite. "Umm umm. Delicious."

I wrinkled my nose.

"Don't do that!" she said. "Be willing to open your horizons and try something new. What appears to be icky at first might turn out to be exactly what you need. You know, that's what your GeeGee used to say. She was always up for an adventure."

"GeeGee?" we both said at once.

"That surprises you, eh?" She laughed. "She liked to play that little old lady card, said it helped her get away with things. But she was like a wild colt when you let her out of the stable."

"Sounds like you knew her well," I said.

"Friends for decades!" she proudly announced, taking out her finger guns with a bang, bang. Then blowing off the ends and putting them back in her imaginary holsters.

"I'm sorry you lost your friend," I said sadly.

"Eh, eh, eh." She wiggled a finger at me. "GeeGee said no pity parties. She'd hate that. She said just get on with it. So I am."

Groceries put away, we joined Zell at the table.

"You said you're here about the book club," Glo started. "Did you see our flyer?"

"I did! Stopped by the grocery and spotted it right off. Did a little jig right there in the store. Some young kiddo joined me, and we had a fine little dance off."

I smiled at the vision that popped in my head. "You want to join our book club?"

"I've been in the book club for ages! Was just waiting for you to arrive and open her back up again."

"That's wonderful!" I reached over and patted her arm. "Our very first official member."

"Not so," she said. "You and Glo would be the first two. But I'll take the number three spot, thank you very much! Better check your messages and approve the others."

I picked up my phone and saw that I had a dozen new texts from unknown numbers.

"Would these be people who were in the club before?" Glo asked.

"Heck no. All those folks went on to a better place. We let the group dwindle down. Was just me and GeeGee left. Then *poof* she was gone, so now it's just me. Read the messages! Who we got comin'?"

We spent the next hour texting back and forth with the new people. We sorted out the dozen applicants and weeded out those who weren't ready to commit. It appeared we had our group of eight all set for Saturday.

7

"I made breakfast!" Glo looked positively radiant. "To celebrate book club day!"

I tried very hard to look happy about another of Glo's home-cooked meals, then I thought of the book club and felt a genuine smile light up my face.

"Ta-da!" She gestured to the kitchen table, and I burst out laughing.

"Ahh! Frosted Shredded Wheat! My favorite cereal."

"Did you for one minute think that I believe myself a good cook? I do have taste buds, you know."

"Well, thanks for the breakfast." I gave her a hug. "I smell coffee, too."

"Only the best for my favorite niece."

"Your only niece. Man, that is the oldest joke in the book."

I sat down at the table and poured cereal into my bowl. Glo brought over the coffee pot, sugar, and creamer.

"I tell everyone I like coffee, but you know what I really love is sugar and creamer." I was excited to open the new flavor. "Cinnamon Vanilla Cream. Yum."

"I'm well aware of your habit. That's why I bought three of those. Can I try?"

I hugged the bottle to my chest. "I don't know. If we only have three ..."

She wrestled the bottle out of my hands and made a big show of adding it to her cup.

"After breakfast do you want to get started on the food for the potluck?" Glo asked.

"Sounds good." I heard a knock on the door. "It's so early. Who could that be?"

I opened the front door, but no one was there. There was another knock.

"It's coming from the basement door, or I guess we should call it the library door, huh?"

I opened the door to see Frank standing there with a wooden backscratcher in his mouth.

"Pttt." He spit out the backscratcher. "A bit clumsy, I know. But it works." He waltzed into the kitchen as if he owned the place. He jumped up onto the counter. He arched his back, stretched his legs, and give a huge yawn.

"Would love a touch of that cinnamon creamer in my coffee," he said. "Smells divine."

"You drink coffee?" Glo asked.

"Every morning. Gets the old motor running."

I shook my head. "It's not good for you."

He stretched his neck and made a show of looking into our two cups.

"Yeah, but we're people," I said.

He gasped. "You're *people!* I had no idea!" He put a paw over his chest.

Glo laughed and filled a small saucer with creamer and just a drop of coffee.

"Keep pouring, toots," said Frank.

She added more coffee.

"Uhh uhh."

She added another dose.

"That'll do. Many thanks, dear girl."

Glo started to put the saucer on the floor.

"What am I, a barbarian? I'll join you at the table." Frank jumped up onto the table, leaping right over my cereal bowl.

"Heh. Nice jumpin' there Frank," he said to himself.

Glo put his saucer down next to him. He leaned over and lapped up a sip then made a groan of pleasure.

"Ahh. So, what's our plan for the day, ladies?"

Glo and I looked at each other and smiled. Seemed like we were now a trio.

"We're setting up for the book club. Making food for the potluck."

"I vote for tuna fish sandwiches," said Frank. "Speaking of food. Who would like to make me some breakfast?"

"I got it." I stood up and walked toward the refrigerator. "Cat food, shrimp, or salmon?"

"Yes, please." Frank licked his lips.

~ ~ ~

We were elbow-deep in making tuna fish sandwiches, turkey sandwiches, and macaroni salad when the gong of the doorbell sounded. I glanced at the clock. It wasn't even eleven yet, and our first book club meeting didn't start until noon.

"Maybe it's Theo?" I grabbed a towel and wiped off my hands on the way to the door.

I opened the door to a woman dressed in black jeans and a black leather jacket. She had black leather gloves and a helmet in her hands. She wore a bandana on her head and had two long brunette braids hanging out the bottom. I could see a blue and green feather tattoo near her left ear. Behind her, parked *on my lawn* was an all-black motorcycle.

"Yo," she said.

"Hi, can I help you?"

"This the book club place?" she asked.

"Yes, it is."

"I'm Vee."

"Hmm. I don't have anyone on my list named Vee."

"Yeah, it's Valentina. Here." She held a piece of paper toward me. "I need to get this signed, and if I don't do it now, I might forget."

"Come on in," I didn't take the paper, but pulled the door open, and she followed me to the kitchen.

"Hey, Glo. This is Valentina."

"It's Vee," she said. She gave a half-hearted wave to Glo.

"I'm Glo. It's G-l-o, short for Gloria."

"Cool."

The cat cleared his throat in that odd manly way.

"And this is Frank. Our library cat."

Vee plopped herself down on the floor and reached over to pet Frank. He purred and rubbed his head along her hand.

"See, now that's how you properly greet a Siamese," said Frank.

"Whoa. The cat talks." She nodded her head. "Cool." She continued to pet Frank.

I had to give her a lot of credit. She calmly accepted Frank as if he weren't an overconfident talking cat with a manly voice.

"Would you like a cup of coffee, Vee?" Glo offered.

"Yeah, sure."

"You're early," I said. "Book club doesn't start for another hour."

"So? Is this like Buckingham Palace or something? You got a problem with me being early?"

"Umm. No, that's fine. We're just preparing the lunch."

Vee glanced at the counter. "I know how to make a sandwich. Should I help?"

"That would be great," said Glo. She pushed a loaf of bread, turkey, and vegetables to the other side of the counter. "Have at it."

"You said something about paperwork?" I reminded Vee.

She pulled the envelope out of her back pocket and handed it to me.

"What is this?" I asked.

"It's a court order. Judge says I gotta be here for every meeting."

"You were *court ordered* to join the book club?" I pulled out the paper and looked at the formal document. "Can I ask what happened?"

"Yeah sure. Otherwise, you'll all be making up rubbish in your heads." Vee had jumped right in. She washed her hands and got busy making turkey sandwiches. She spoke as she worked.

"I came home early from work. My boyfriend's bike was there, but there was another bike. I knew who it belonged to since it had a ridiculous pink fairy painted on the gas tank. It was Stiletto's."

"Stiletto, as in the shoe?" Glo asked.

"Her real name's Stephanie. So, I go inside the house. By the sounds coming from upstairs in our bedroom I could tell they weren't playing cards, if you know what I mean."

Glo let out a low whistle. I gasped and nodded. Frank was clicking his tongue.

"I walked into my room. Went right past them, I did. Didn't say a word. Grabbed my suitcase and threw a bunch of stuff in it. They huddled in the bed like the snakes they were. Then I left."

"Wow, that was brave of you," I said.

"Way to go, girlfriend!" said Frank.

"Yeah, well. I lit their bikes on fire on my way out."

"You *lit their motorcycles on fire!*" Glo was staring at her.

"Gutsy." Frank hooted.

Vee shrugged. "Oh, don't look so horrified. They were in the garage. He had a sprinkler system, so it's not like I burned down the house or anything. When the fire alarm started shrieking, I left, and never looked back.

"Got arrested, of course. The judge said that her friend Clara something-or-other had this book club. I had a choice. A year in jail or a year in this club. So, makes sense I chose the club, right? When I saw your flyer in the store, I figured I best get started so I don't run out of time. So, where's this Clara? She needs to sign the paper."

"Clara has passed away," I said, and Frank made a choking sound. "I'm sorry, he's probably grieving. It didn't happen that long ago. My Aunt Glo and I run the club now. But I'm happy to sign if that works?"

"Yeah, sure, I guess," said Vee, putting together another sandwich. "Thanks." I realized with a start that she'd made about ten sandwiches while she told us her story.

8

We were setting up the sandwiches, fruit, and brownies on trays when Zelda — oh, now Zell – came waltzing into the kitchen.

"Door was open," she said by way of greeting. She was holding several plastic containers.

"I thought you said folks here don't go into homes where they don't belong?" Glo quoted her comment from when we first met her.

"Yeah, and I belong. Book club member," she pointed to herself, then placed her containers on the counter. "Book club day." She twirled her finger in the air. "Book club location." She pointed to the door that led downstairs.

"I was just teasing," said Glo in a soft voice.

Zell laughed. "No worries, little glow worm. I'm good. It takes a heck of a lot more than that to bother me. Who're you?" She scrutinized Vee with a look of curiosity.

"Vee."

"V like the letter V? Or Vee like some kind of nickname?"

"I guess both the letter and a nickname."

"I have one of those now, too!" She smiled, showing off her bionic teeth and darling dimples. "Zell is short for Zelda. So, it's you, me, and Glo with the awesome nicknames. Poor little Paige here doesn't have one. We don't want to call her Pee now do we?"

Zell and Vee both had a good laugh over that, then bumped fists. I saw the start of an unlikely friendship. Two very different women, yet both of them blunt, saying whatever popped into their brains without reservation. They would be lively book club members, that was for sure.

Zell spotted Frank and hustled over to him. "Frank! Good to see you, honey. How's my favorite feline?"

"Doin' fine Zelda. How're you?

"Oh, it's Zell now. My new nickname. Like it?"

"Love it, actually." He lifted his paw, and they had a funny little fist bump.

"What's with all the fist bumping around here?" I asked.

"It's the Nickname Club secret handshake," said Frank. They all laughed.

The gong of the doorbell sounded through the house.

"Doorbell!" announced Zell, as if her bionic hearing allowed her to hear something we all missed.

I opened the door to see a tall, beefy man dressed in a turquoise plaid shirt, beige khakis, and white Keds. I could see magenta-colored socks peeking out. He was clean-shaven and his hair was expertly styled. He was holding a large cake carrier with a red handle.

"Good afternoon." His voice was deep and formal. "I'm here for the book club meeting. Sebastian Mendoza."

"Hi, Sebastian! I'm Paige. We texted. Please come in."

"Thank you. Am I the first to arrive?" He looked worried.

"Oh, no, you're not. Everyone's in the kitchen."

He looked relieved not to have broken some rule about arriving early. He'd have to teach that one to Vee. I stepped aside and invited him in.

"Oh, my goodness! Your home is fabulous!" The formal voice evaporated in his enthusiasm. "Just look at this fireplace!" He scuttled over and ran has hand over the rock face. "Oh, and this darling lamp. Love it. And the view of the lake. Ahhh!" He ran over to the window and leaned on the ledge with both elbows, his chin on his fists, peering outside. "Love-Love-Loving it!"

"Thank you. We love it, too. Want to meet everyone? It's right this way." I got his attention and led him into the kitchen. "Hey, everyone. This is Sebastian."

"Hi, people!" He gave a wave to the group. "I brought cake!" He held up his offering and then put it on the counter.

"You got a nickname Sebastian?" Zell asked as she walked over and stood about two inches in front of him.

"No, ma'am. Just Sebastian." He looked down on the spitfire octogenarian with a smile.

She looked back up at him and squinted her eyes. Then she nodded. "Welcome to the book club, Sebastian. I'm eighty. Just turned. No filters. Be forewarned."

"Consider me suitably forewarned." He gave her a salute. He looked very serious, but I could see cheerful crinkles at the corners of his mouth and eyes.

Frank walked slowly up to Sebastian and sat in front of him. He looked up and meowed. I wondered if it was some kind of test.

Sebastian put his hands to his cheeks and let out a happy squeal. "I *looove* Siamese cats! Oh, and you are a beauty, aren't you! Simply magnificent." He leaned down and ran a hand down Frank's back. "Ahhh. And as soft as a feather you are, my lovely."

"Thank you, Sebastian. That was very kind," said

Frank.

"Ohhh!" squeaked Sebastian. "Did everyone hear that?" His head spun as he looked around the room. Everyone nodded. "The cat talks!" He clapped his hands. "Oh, my word! What fun! So glad I joined this book club. I'm having a good time already."

The gong announced another arrival and this time Glo went to answer it. She came back into the room with a petite Asian woman. Her green polka-dotted dress was set off by a wide white belt and a patterned scarf. White patent-leather boots accented her small feet. Long, glossy black hair with wispy sideswept bangs set off her delicate features. She looked like a miniature fashion model. Her large, round glasses made her eyes look huge. She was holding a tray of appetizers that was almost as big as she was. I took the tray from her and added it to the mounting collection of food on the counter.

"Allow me to introduce Emiko," said Glo.

"Nope, nope, nope. I don't think so," said Frank, leaving Sebastian and walking up to Emiko. He shook his head. "You don't look like an Emiko to me. You need a more ... trendy name. I'm going to call you ... Kisaragi."

I was horrified that Frank had welcomed her in this manner and stepped forward to try to smooth it over. I needn't have worried though. She knelt down to him and held her own. Not only was I surprised at her suave reply, but she also didn't seem the least bit bothered that the cat was talking.

"Isn't Honey Kisaragi an Anime character?" she asked the cat. "A teenager who is turned into a super android?"

"Exactly right! See, I knew you were smart. You

seem like a covert superhero to me."

"Well, I'm way older than sixteen."

"She's chronologically over 100," Frank said. "Not that I'm saying you look old, cuz what are you, maybe twenty? Honey Kisaragi is brilliant, carefree, and perky – just like you. And with those big round eyes you look just like her."

"These are glasses." She tapped her frames. "And I'm twenty-five. But … thank you, cat."

"My pleasure. And the name's Frank."

"Good to meet you, Frank. I must say, I don't care for Kisaragi. How about Koko? That's what my family calls me."

"I like it!" Frank turned to the group. "Another fine nickname. Paige, you are in the minority around here. If you want, I'm sure I could come up with something for you."

"No, thanks," I replied, "I'll be fine with Paige."

"It's your call," he said. He looked around the room. "Hey. We have two more members coming. Tell us what to expect, will ya?"

"Sure. It's a mother and her son. Apparently, the father is involved in international business and going out of town for a month, and the mom doesn't want to leave him alone."

"Is he a little child?" Zell looked shocked. "Not sure that's wise."

"No. Apparently, he's a teenager, but prone to … mischief when the parents aren't around. Therefore, he'll be here with us."

"Soooo. He's grounded," said Frank.

"I didn't say that."

"How much you wanna bet?" Frank looked as smug as a cat could. "Names?"

"Uhhh. The mother is Moonbeam."

There was a snicker around the room, though

everyone tried to hold it back.

I heard Emiko whisper to Glo, "Is Moonbeam a name?"

"And the son?" asked Sebastian.

"Forrest."

"Oh, this ought to be real good," said Frank.

A knock at the door announced our final members. I walked out of the kitchen, and everyone scooted around behind me and was staring at the door. I turned around and faced them. "Stop it, you guys. Go back in the kitchen and act normal." As if I knew what normal was with this bunch.

They all started chatting animatedly to each other in nonsense and pretending not to look at the door. I covered my mouth with my hand so they couldn't see me smile. I was so darn happy to see this eccentric group of people so quickly becoming friends. Even if it took a hippie and her son to pull it all together.

The minute I opened the door I knew they were going to have a heyday with this. Moonbeam was a vision in a flowing flower-power kaftan. Her frizzy brown hair was liberally touched with gray and tucked into a tie-dyed headband. The macrame necklace and matching earrings she wore screamed homemade. On her feet: brown sandals that showed off her unpainted toenails that looked like they'd been working in the garden all morning. She was holding four reusable produce bags filled with fruits and vegetables.

Moonbeam's son Forrest looked like any normal, bored teenager. Black hair in an untidy Afro, a ripped t-shirt and what was probably a favorite pair of old jeans. He was carrying a blender. Ah, not a blender. A juicer.

"Welcome!" I smiled warmly at this unique twosome. "Come right in. You must be Moonbeam and Forrest."

"That's amazing! How did you guess?" said Moonbeam.

Forrest rolled his eyes.

We stepped into the kitchen, and I shut my eyes, saying a silent prayer. I was so glad I asked the group to act normal. As Moonbeam and Forrest came through the door, the group was acting anything but normal. They were lined up against the kitchen island all facing the door. Zell jabbed Vee in the arm and whispered, much too loudly, "Told ya."

I ignored their behavior and introduced our newest members. "This is Moonbeam and Forrest."

"Peace and Namaste," said Zell.

Sebastian put his hands in a prayer position and bowed to them. "My soul recognizes your soul."

Vee and Emiko held up their hands in peace signs.

It took everything in me not to bang my head against the wall.

Moonbeam, however, looked eager and enthralled by the group. She put her bags down and spread her arms wide to the room. "Greetings, lovely people. Happy to meet you, one and all!"

Frank walked up to Moonbeam and stood in front of her. He tipped his head side to side, as if to analyze her. "Well, then. Are you a hippie?" he asked.

Moonbeam let out an excited squeak. "Psychedelic!" she hooted.

Forrest glanced over at this mother, then looked

down at the cat. He shrugged then pulled his phone out of his pocket and commenced with scrolling.

Moonbeam looked at the cat with wide eyes. "Consider my mind officially blown." She sat down on the floor in front of Frank. "No, not a hippie. I simply disassociate from the cultural movement. A nonconformist, if you will."

"So then, you even non-confirm with your hippie counterparts?" Frank asked.

"Well said, little man. As you non-conform with your breed, I see."

"Well said, big woman."

Moonbeam shook with laughter. "Oh, this is going to be so fun. I knew it!" She looked up at her son. "Didn't I tell you so, Forrest?"

He mumbled "Umm, hmm," but I noticed he was surfing TikTok on his phone.

Moonbeam stood up in one fluid yoga-type movement. "Is this the whole group, then?"

"Yes, this is everyone," I said. I introduced her all around. The *peace, love, and Zen* greetings made me grind my teeth, but Moonbeam seemed more honored than embarrassed.

We commenced with uncovering all the food dishes and spent a good hour getting to know each other. The chatter was constant except for times when Moonbeam was using her juicer to make remarkably delicious smoothies.

I was floored by the easy comradery among this diverse group of people. Perhaps that was due to Cascade Valley being such a small community. I'd learned that when there are less than five thousand people in a town everyone seems to get along.

Glo came over and threw her arm around my shoulders. "A successful beginning, wouldn't you say? Should we corral the horses and head downstairs for our first official book club meeting?”

9

Having seven other people pitch in to clean the kitchen made it take at least twice as long as if I'd done it myself. Having a vocal cat underfoot calling out directions made it worse. However, they all insisted on helping, so here I was, weaving through a crowd to get to the sink. At long last the kitchen was cleaner than it had been before they arrived. Social hour was over; it was time to hit the books.

I grabbed the key, and everyone gathered at the door to the library stairs.

"This is momentous!" declared Sebastian. "I feel like we should have an announcement or a proclamation of some sort."

Glo looked at him proudly and nodded. She loved the drama and was all for a celebration.

Moonbeam began to chant. Forrest rolled his eyes. Zell began to beat out a drumroll on the coffee table. She was surprisingly good. Glo, Vee, and Emiko called out a countdown. "Five ... four ... three ... two ... one!"

I turned the key in the lock and pushed open the door. They started to cheer but I held up my hand. "We're not there yet."

Everyone followed me down the first flight of stairs.

"Now?" asked Emiko.

"Not quite yet," answered Zell. She was happy to be someone in the know.

I opened the second door and my parade followed me down to the bottom of the staircase where we encountered another locked door. I slipped the key in the lock. "Now we're here," I announced.

"Wait!" yelled Zell. She commenced with another drumroll, this time on the wall.

Moonbeam began her chant. Forrest returned to eye-rolling.

Glo, Vee, Emiko, and Sebastian called out another countdown, with just as much enthusiasm as the first time. "Five ... four ... three ... two ... one!"

I turned the key, then slowly opened the door. I waved my hand toward the room and said, "Introducing ... the library!"

The book club members nearly stumbled over each other as they entered the vast space. They were in awe of the amazing room, their heads turning in every direction. I understood that feeling. I still could not believe that all this lived under the inn.

Sebastian ran over to the fireplace with the statue displayed on the mantle. "This is a mirror image of the fireplace upstairs! Does the flue run all the way up through the house, do you suppose? This stonework is pristine."

"Look at this!" Emiko was inspecting the globe. She reached out to twirl it.

"Don't touch that Koko!" Frank stopped her with a firm voice.

"Why not?" she asked.

"It's umm. Fragile. Easily broken. Priceless."

"Oh, okay," said Emiko. She pulled her hand back and wandered over to join Sebastian in his inspection of the statue on top of the fireplace.

Once the group was satisfied with their exploration of the unique library, I gathered them in the seating area where Zell and Frank were already seated and chatting. As they'd been a part of the book club previously, they were already familiar with the library.

"Our first order of business is to select our inaugural book," I announced.

The group cheered.

Glo was standing next to me, and I whispered, "I haven't seen this much enthusiasm since I played softball in Little League."

Glo laughed, then turned away and cheered along with the groups, lifting her hands as if at a rock concert. The only ones not yelling were me and Forrest, who was glued to his phone screen.

"Okay, okay!" I laughed and clapped until I got their attention. "This library contains all mystery books."

"Hopefully cozies," said Moonbeam. "I don't go in for the blood and gore."

"Yes, actually, all cozy mysteries, you'll be happy to know."

"Hopefully lots of paranormal stuff," said Emiko. "I love werewolves, vampires, ghosts—"

"Oh, yeah," said Vee. "Me too."

"I don't know, we haven't explored the titles yet. As my flyer explained," I got us back on track, "the group will read a book together and we'll solve the mystery in our weekly gatherings. We'll agree on the number of chapters, but no reading ahead! It'll be more fun if we sort through the clues, suspects, and red herrings together."

The eager beavers were on the edge of their seats and nodding excitedly.

Glo and I had reviewed our plan for today, so she spoke next. "All the mysteries are shelved in sets of eight books. Don't untie them, please, but each of you bring a set back to the seating area, then we'll vote on our first book."

The gang dispersed as if they were horses at the

opening gate. Sebastian and Vee went up the circular staircase, and I could see them heading off in different directions at the top. Everyone else was perusing the bookcases on the main level. It didn't take long for everyone to return to the seating area, each with a twine-tied stack of books.

"Don't undo the twine on your set until it's your turn," I explained. "We'll examine the cover, and review the description, then decide if it's an option. Oh, and don't read the book club notes that are on top."

"Okay, yeah," said Frank. "Let's call them book club notes."

Zell snorted.

Glo gave them a confused look, then said, "Let's have Paige start us off. What did you find, Paige?"

I picked up my stack. "This one looks fun. It's called, *Shifting the Blame: Murder in a Small Town with a Big Secret.*" I untied the stack, set aside the notes, and held up the book, turning it so everyone could see the cover.

"Oooo!" said Sebastian. "Gorgeous cover! I love small town mysteries."

"Me too," said Zell. "And 'secret' is an excellent title word. It indicates an intriguing plot."

"There's a horse on the cover," pointed out Emiko. "I love to ride, so I like the theme."

"There's no blurb on the back cover, so how about I read the first page?" I asked.

"Good idea," said Glo.

"Bad idea," said Frank, shaking his head vigorously.

"Maybe. Maybe not," said Zell looking at Frank. "Might as well get started, right?"

"I s'pose," said Frank, lifting his little cat shoulders in a shrug.

"Just the first page," said Vee. "I don't care for

listening to a book. I much prefer reading it."

"The first page is fine," Sebastian piped up. "How else will we pick from all these glorious choices!" He gestured around the grand room stuffed to the brim with mysteries.

"Okay then." I cleared my throat and using a dramatic voice, I started to read.

"The crochety old recluse, Randall Ward, hated people. He especially hated those who walked on his land. He spotted the group of people walking in the back forty near his metal fence. They were likely tourists, looking for the trailhead and lost. He'd run out of patience for these kinds of trespassers long ago.

"Randall grabbed his gun and ran outside. He hollered, 'Hey! Get off my property or I'll shoot!' He pulled the trigger and released a warning shot into the air.

"The bunch of tourists jumped and nearly trampled each other, all turning in different directions. Randall chuckled at the scene, then lifted his gun again ..."

"Look at the globe!" gasped Moonbeam.

The globe that Frank had warned Emiko not to touch had turned gold. It was glowing and spinning and shooting sparks.

"Oh, my God!" shrieked Sebastian. "Look!" He pointed behind me. "The library's on fire!"

I turned around to see a large plume of smoke that appeared to be coming out of the back of my chair. I stood up, dropped my stack of books on the floor and yelled, "Somebody call 911!"

"Got it!" yelled Forrest. For once I was glad that he had his phone in hand.

"Help! Help! I can't see anything!" yelled

Sebastian wildly waving his arms. "There's too much smoke!"

"Sebastian! Stop screaming!" yelled Vee. "Everyone! Slowly move toward the door. Hold on to each other as you go."

The room quickly filled up with smoke until we couldn't see a thing. We were reaching out toward each other and slowly inching toward where we assumed the door to be, but it seemed to be much farther away than I remembered. I began to panic. Were we getting disoriented from the smoke? Were we turned around and heading away from the door and into the stacks? Did I invite all these people to my new home only for all of us to perish in a fire?

10

As quickly as the smoke had filled the room it began to dissipate. Several of the members where coughing. We were all waving our hands in front of our faces to clear the smoke.

Frank mumbled "Uh oh" under his breath, but I clearly heard him.

I looked down at the cat. "Frank, what do you—" I gasped when I looked back up. We were no longer in the library. We were standing in an open field in front of a high metal fence.

Everyone began to talk at once.

"What happened?"

"Where are we?"

"This is impossible!"

"Have we been drugged?"

A loud gunshot rang out through the air. A man off in the distance yelled, "Hey! I told you to get off my property! I'll shoot ya. I ain't kiddin'."

Frank looked at Zell. "Oops." Then he turned toward the rest of us. "Guess we forgot to tell you all something."

We all turned to stare at Frank.

"What on earth is happening?" screeched Sebastian, holding his hands to the sides of his face.

Zell looked at Frank. "I got this," she said to him. "Well, here's the thing—"

Another gunshot rang out and a bullet hit a tree not far from where we were standing. "Get moving!" hollered the man.

"Run!" yelled Zell.

She and Frank began to run away from the sound of the shouting man. Sebastian sat down on the grass, put his head in his hands and started to cry.

Frank and Zell spun back around toward us. "Come on!" yelled Zell.

Vee grabbed Sebastian by the arm and yelled, "Get up! Now! Run!"

The man in the distance was still shouting. "That's right! Get the heck outta here! And don't come back." He fired his gun again, hitting another tree nearby.

Sebastian screamed and fell back to the ground in a frightened heap. Vee pulled him by one arm, and Emiko grabbed his other. They yanked him up off the ground.

"Aim for the break in the fence!" Zell yelled.

After a few false starts with people going in the wrong direction, we were all finally running toward a broken part of the metal fence. One by one we squeezed through the space until we were all clustered together.

We could still hear the crazy man shouting at us. He punctuated his words with another shot.

Vee pointed to an old barn not far from where we were standing. "Head for the barn!" she yelled.

We all ran to the structure. It took three of us to slide the heavy wooden door open. It creaked from lack of use, but we finally had it open wide enough for all of us to get inside.

Zell, Glo, and I were gasping for air. Sebastian was leaned over, his hands on his thighs, trying to catch his breath. Vee, Emiko, Moonbeam, and Forrest looked like they'd just taken a stroll through town. The cat was sitting on the ground grooming his tail. It was clear which members of this group were in shape, and which weren't. Sadly, I wasn't in the fit category; my daily mile on the treadmill had not prepared me for this.

When we all caught our breath, we turned to stare at Frank and Zell, the two who were involved with the book club before we took it over.

"What?" asked Frank, moving from grooming his tail to cleaning his paws.

"You know what!" I said in a much louder voice than I intended. "Tell us what is happening!"

"Well, isn't that obvious?" he said. "We're in the book."

11

"We're in the book?!" My words were echoed by everyone except Zell, who clearly was privy to the whole thing.

"Yeah, well. I tried to warn you," said Frank.

"Warn us?" My voice came out shrill and loud. I was stunned by his casual comment.

"When?" Vee chimed in, standing with her hands on her hips.

Frank looked annoyed. "I said 'that's not a good idea.' And then I said 'oops.'"

"I remember that. He did say it wasn't a good idea," agreed Moonbeam, nodding so vigorously her curls bounced. Forrest glanced at his mother with a look of bewilderment, then he rolled his eyes. He didn't pull out his phone, though.

"And he did say 'oops'," said Zell.

"That's true. I remember. He said 'oops'," Moonbeam added.

"Oh, my gosh!" Sebastian's voice got an octave higher with each word. "That's not even close to a warning! You could have—"

Zell interrupted him and held up her hand. "Let's not have this conversation here," she said.

"And where exactly should we have this conversation?" asked Vee.

"At the inn, of course," said Zell.

"What inn?" Glo asked.

"Why, your inn. The Snapdragon, of course. You know, the one that used to belong to GeeGee?"

"Oh. joy! We can go home!" Sebastian clapped his

hands and looked extremely relieved.

“We should skirt the backside of the building, out of eyesight of Randall Ward,” said Zell.

Vee’s brows knit in confusion, and I asked the question I was sure was in her mind. “How do you know the shooter next door is named Randall Ward?”

“Weren’t you listening to the book?” Zell asked. “It said *‘the crochety old recluse, Randall Ward, shot at them.’*”

“Well, at that point I had no idea I’d be *in the book*,” snarled Vee. “Perhaps if I knew that bit of helpful information, I would have paid closer attention.” She stepped one long stride closer to Zell.

Emiko put her hand on Vee’s arm. “Hey. Let’s stay united. We’re all in this together now.”

“Good point, Koko!” said Frank.

“If I were you, I’d keep your little kitty lips sealed,” said Vee.

“Hurmmph,” said Frank, keeping his lips together.

“So how do we get home?” Emiko asked.

“You can follow me ... umm ... *to the inn*,” said Zell, enunciating every word.

The group followed Zell out of the barn door. Frank was trailing at the end of the line, still miffed after being scolded by Vee.

Zell led us around the barn. She looked around and then she trotted across an apple orchard. She seemed to up the level of spry since we entered the book. As we reached the other side of the trees, a building loomed on the knoll ahead of us ... our house.

“No freakin’ way,” said Vee.

“Our house followed us here?” Glo started to laugh. “That is ridiculous!”

"And the rest of this is not ridiculous?" I pointed out.

"You said we could go *home*," Sebastian whined, pointing at Zell with a shaky finger.

"Young man, I never lie. I said we could go to the inn. I specifically never used the word *home*." Zell looked affronted at his accusation.

Glo interrupted their argument. "Seriously, guys! Look at that! It's our house! It came with us!" Glo was still laughing that joyful belly laugh she had when something really struck her funny bone.

Glo's laugh was contagious, and soon we had all joined her. Of course, part of that was an emotional release due to the fact we'd been enveloped by smoke, sucked into a book, shot at by a crazy man, and run for our lives.

We could barely walk, for all our laughter. I noticed that even Forrest was chuckling, although he tried to hide it.

"Let's pick up the pace, people!" Zell was now marching rapidly toward the house. Our house that was located on a knoll, in the country, next door to an apple orchard. In a book.

~ ~ ~

It was disorienting to be in our kitchen, making a pot of coffee, and pulling leftovers from the potluck out of our refrigerator – all while looking out the window at an unfamiliar apple orchard.

"Anyone want a smoothie?" asked Moonbeam.

"Me!" Emiko raised her hand.

"Would love just a small one," added Zell, holding

up her hand and pinching her fingers an inch apart.

"Ohhh, yes please!" said Glo. "Your smoothies are truly amazing."

"Thank you, sunshine." Moonbeam smiled as she gathered up the ingredients.

The group operated so smoothly in my kitchen that it seemed they'd been friends for years – not just hours. A lot had happened to us today. I think our adrenaline was still pumping.

We organized the leftovers, re-heated what needed warming, and lined up plates, bowls, and silverware. Everyone was starving and our plates were soon overflowing. I noticed that Forrest hadn't been so engaged on his phone, he even loaded up a plate for Frank. The large group didn't fit in the kitchen booth, of course, so we carried our plates over to the eating nook.

"I think it's time for Zell and Frank to tell us what we're in for," Glo said as she took a seat.

Frank jumped up on a chair, and Forrest put the plate he'd prepared for the cat right in front of him on the table. I assumed we were now all casually accepting the fact that the talking cat would be treated as one of the group, which led me to think of the eight seats in the library and eight books in the twine bundle.

"I was just thinking, why are there eight books in the bundle if we left the books behind?"

"Oh, the books are a ... umm ... what would you call it, Frank"? Zell asked.

He tilted his head in thought. "A keepsake? A summary?"

"Ooo, good word. A summary, yes. It wouldn't be any fun if we knew the story ahead of time, would it?"

"Yessss, it would!" hissed Sebastian. "Then we would have known not to go in the field where we would be shot at!" He started to shake, his anxiety evident.

Moonbeam got up from her seat and stood behind him. She put her hands on his shoulders. "Breathe with me," she said in a soothing voice. "Innnn. Ooout." She gently massaged his shoulders, which had risen all the way up to his ears with tension. She continued the exercise until Sebastian became calm and relaxed.

He reached up and patted her hand. "Thanks, Moonbeam. I'm okay now."

Frank had been happily munching on his meal, and he finally looked up from his plate. "Delish! Who's ready to hear the book club rules!"

"Well, I wouldn't exactly call them rules. There're no rules." said Zell. "More like ... guidelines."

"Guess you're right," said Frank. "Perhaps procedures might be a better description."

"Ah! That's a good one. Procedures—"

"Excuse me!" Vee interrupted. "Don't think the label matters. Can you give us the scoop?"

"Even better!" said Frank. "The scoop!"

Zell nodded. "The scoop." She popped the P at the end of the word.

We all looked at the two of them expectantly.

"You go ahead and start, Frankie."

"No, no. Ladies first, Zell."

"Just tell us already!" hollered Forrest.

The room got quiet as we all tried not to look at Forrest. But I heard several chuckles around the table.

"I'll start," said Frank. "We're in a book."

There was a mass groan around the table.

"We got there because Paige read the first page." He chuckled. "Paige read a page."

"You're supposed to only read the *blurb* on the back cover of your possible choices," said Zell.

"Everybody picks one, then we read all the *blurbs*. Then the group votes on their choice. Only after you make the choice do you read the first page. Then the globe spins and sparks, and there's that smokey fog thing, and *poof* you're in the book.

"The inn always comes with us. Cuz, I mean, where else are we supposed to stay? That's why there's eight guest suites, we each get one! Well, it's kind of pre-chosen for you, cuz when you get up there, you'll find all your stuff from your own home has been packed in these cool vacuum sealed bags and transferred over. But you can trade rooms, if you want."

"That's magical!" said Glo.

"Bingo!" said Zell. "Lotsa magical stuff goes on. If you haven't already figured that part out."

"Tell them about the worksheets," said Frank.

"Right, those papers you called book club notes are actually ... what is it called, Frank?"

"A murder board?"

"Yeah, it's like the format for the murder board," said Zell. "The book club notes are sort of like clues to help us! Well, uh. Not really clues, more like an outline. We pool our ideas as we move through the book chapters and create a big murder board with the group. The murder board is down in the library. It's where we have our meetings.

"And the coolest part," continued Zell, "Is that you can't leave the book until the mystery is solved!" She clapped her hands.

Sebastian resumed his wailing and hyperventilating.

"Oh, buck up, boy!" said Zell. "It's *fun*."

Emiko raised her hand, as if in class.

"Yes, Emiko?" said Frank.

"Did you ever have trouble solving the mystery?"

"Depends on what you mean by trouble," said

Frank. "One time we were stuck in a book for over a month. It was a challenge, but we finally got it!"

Zell and he both pumped their fists in the air.

"I don't understand," said Vee. "If you are stuck in the book until the mystery is solved, then why do you do this?"

Frank and Zelda both answered together, "Why would you not?"

12

I woke up in my beautiful cherry tree-blossom room and felt a rush of happiness. Sure, we were stuck in a murder mystery book, but I had the weirdest feeling this was going to be an awesome adventure, and I was really up for it.

I knew that Glo, being a morning person, would already have the coffee brewing and the tea kettle full of hot water. When I came down the stairs, I heard voices in the kitchen. I stopped for a moment and realized that Glo had morning company. It sounded like Zell, Moonbeam, and Sebastian.

I paused at the doorway when I heard them laughing. It was a lovely sound to wake up to.

"Good morning fellow sleuths!" I walked in to see the four of them in a circle, bent over in some sort of yoga pose. Of course, the only one who actually looked like she was in a yoga pose was Moonbeam, who was folded in half and grasping her ankles.

"We're doin' a Morning Salute!" said Zell proudly.

"A Sun Salutation," corrected Moonbeam. "And you are looking very good, Zell."

I bit back a laugh, as she looked anything but. Zell was tapping out a drum beat on her knees. She was having fun, even though she looked about to fall over.

"Would you like to join us, Paige?" asked Moonbeam.

"Sure."

We twisted our way through the last few poses, then everyone prepared cups of coffee or tea, and we started rummaging in the pantry and refrigerator for breakfast foods.

"Hey, Zell. Can we go grocery shopping here? Or are we limited to mystery-solving activities?"

"Good question, Paige!" said Glo.

"Oh, yeah. We can shop, go out to dinner, even go to the movies if we want. Solving mysteries isn't a 24/7 job. We live in the book just like all the other characters. 'Cept we're real." Zell chuckled. "But don't tell them that. They wouldn't believe ya anyhow."

Luckily, we'd gone to the store back in the real world, though at the time Glo and I only shopped for the two of us. And a cat. We all worked together to create a breakfast buffet with the ingredients we had on hand. Eggs, pancakes, turkey sausages, toast, yogurt, and Zell's addition of chips and salsa.

"What? I like chips and salsa," she said as she dumped the chips into a bowl, munching on one as she worked.

One by one the rest of the group wandered into the kitchen, sleepily muttering good mornings and filling cups of tea or coffee.

Forrest came into the kitchen last, his hair tamed by a head of braids.

"How on earth did you do all that this morning?" asked Vee, pointing at her own head.

"Mom did it. She's quick," he mumbled.

"I'll say. Looks good," nodded Vee, giving him a thumbs up.

Forrest actually smiled.

Breakfast plates filled, we sat around the dining table, everyone raving about their rooms. I was surprised to learn that Vee had traded rooms so she could have the Japanese garden room. She said it reminded her of the vast open spaces on the road trips she took on her bike.

Sebastian laid a piece of paper on the table. "Attention please," he said. "The book club notes. We should review these."

"I thought you wanted to go home," said Emiko.

"Yeah! I do! That's why we need to get right on this." He tapped on the paper with his finger. "I don't want to be here any longer than I must. Besides, I have a dinner party planned with friends this weekend." He lifted his chin and looked super serious.

"Where'd you get the notes?" asked Vee.

"Down in the library. It was on the coffee table."

"The library wasn't locked?" Glo asked.

"It's never locked when we're in a book," said Zell. "We need full access to the murder board and stuff."

"We're allowed to use the library?" Emiko's eyes shone with excitement.

"Yup," said Zell. "Just don't open the twine sets. Have no idea what might happen if you do that."

A jingling of bells had us all turning toward the door. Frank stood there, shaking a cat toy in his mouth to get our attention. "Pttt." He spit it out on the floor. "Ladies and Gentlemen, fresh from nine blissful hours of sleep ... I give you, the star of the show: Frank!" He took a bow. "Now, who would like the honor of preparing my breakfast?"

We stared at the cat. Nobody moved.

He sat down and looked up at us with sweet, soft kitty eyes. He tilted his head and meowed, a quiet, delicate sound.

Zell, Glo, Sebastian, Emiko, and Forrest all stood up at the same moment.

"Gotcha!" Frank pumped a small furry fist in the air.

They all sat back down.

"Darn it. Sorry, sorry, mew, mee-ow. Meow,

meow?" The last meow came out clearly as a question.

"I got it," said Forrest. He went into the kitchen to fill a plate for Frank.

Sebastian again tapped the paper, his eyes scanning the group. "According to the notes, we need to talk to locals, and explore the area. Figure out who to trust and who to avoid. Then make a list of suspects and begin to discover alibis, determine motive and opportunity, and detect lies."

"Forgetting a tiny little detail," said Frank.

Sebastian looked up from the paper.

Frank closed his eyes and shook his head. "We need to find the dead body first."

Everyone looked stunned.

"We usually find it in the first couple of chapters." Frank announced. "Since we didn't find a body yesterday, that means today's probably the day."

"Yup," said Zell. "I think we're supposed to be on Randall Ward's property. Why else would we land there? We should go back after breakfast."

~ ~ ~

I absolutely could not believe that the group of us were stomping through the orchard adjacent to the property of a man who'd yelled and shot at us yesterday. This was so the opposite of any rational decision I'd ever made in my life. Yet, it seemed to be the only plan of action to escape from the book, based on our two experts. I was a bit concerned that our "experts" were a talking cat and a wildly uninhibited octogenarian.

"Let's get over to the barn so we can see more clearly," said Vee. She was wearing binoculars around her neck.

"Vee! Where did you get those binoculars?" I asked.

She shrugged her shoulders. "In my room. Figured they'd come in handy."

Zell patted her on the back. "Good thinking, young lady."

Vee's mouth turned up on in a half smile at the phrase "young lady."

We hiked through the grass, ducking behind trees as we went.

"Not sure what all the hiding behind trees is going to do for you," said Frank. "There's like eighteen of you clowns."

"Only eight," said Zell. "Always eight. Until it's not. You know that, Frank."

"Eight, eighteen. Whatever. We're about as inconspicuous as a bull in a china shop."

"I think that means you knock stuff over," said Zell.

"Um, then inconspicuous as a snowstorm? How's that?"

"Better," Zell answered.

I coughed to gain their attention. "Maybe one of us should get closer to the fence with the binoculars to look for signs of Randall Ward?"

Vee handed her binoculars to Forrest. "Since you're wearing camouflage, do you mind?"

"Sure." He took the binoculars and crept on his hands and knees over to the fence. I glanced at Moonbeam. She was biting her nails, her face a mask of worry, but she didn't stop her son's reconnaissance. I gave her credit for that.

Forrest scanned the property next door from right to left, then back again. He stood up and motioned us over.

We gathered at the fence.

"I don't see any movement over there," said Forrest. "And the house is dark. Blinds closed. Maybe he sleeps late?"

"Good job, Jungle," said Frank.

Glo leaned down and whispered, "Forrest."

"Ah, yeah, of course. I mean Forrest."

Without having to call it out, we all walked over to the broken part of the fence that we'd squeezed through yesterday. One by one we passed through to the other side.

"Should we explore in groups?" Emiko asked.

"Good idea," said Moonbeam. "Safety in numbers."

"If you see something we should know about, just whistle and hold up your hands," said Glo.

"Can't whistle," said Zell. "Should I sing, instead?"

"Um, I figured we'd be more discreet," said Glo. "How about if you clap your hands?"

"Gotcha."

We split up and began to make our way around the property and toward the house. I saw Sebastian and Emiko peering into windows, trying to see around the closed blinds. They were being awfully brave.

I had somehow managed to be paired up with Frank. I admit, he was good at slinking around, being a cat and all.

Frank began sniffing the air. "Something smells weird. This way."

I followed him to an old shed near the house. There was a rancid smell coming from the area. I plugged my nose and started to circle the shed.

"What's this?" I whispered.

"Looks like a metal cage," said Frank, not in a whisper at all.

I moved closer and removed a branch that was obscuring most of the cage.

Then I heard a loud scream. I quickly realized that the scream had come from me.

The group came running in my direction. I screamed again, tossed the branch down and ran in the opposite direction.

Glo caught up with me and took me by the arms. She looked me in the eye, "Paige! Why are you screaming?"

I stopped screaming and was gasping for air. "Over there. By the shed."

She turned around to see what I was pointing to.

"No! Don't look! It's awful!"

"Of course we have to look," said Zell. "I'm guessin' you found the dead body."

13

Zell had no hesitation. She stomped over to the see what I'd found. She leaned over with her hands on her hips and stared at the cage. "Yeppers. One dead body!"

"Alright!" said Frank, pumping one furry paw in the air. "Let's get this party started."

I gasped at their casual responses. "What is wrong with you two? It's a dead man!"

"Oh, honey," said Zell. "He's just a character in a book. Well, was a character. That was his part. Yell. Shoot. Die."

"He's not *real*," said Frank, snickering.

"He certainly looked real yesterday," said Sebastian. "When he was *shooting at us*."

"As far as we know, those aren't real bullets, and nobody could die."

"What do you mean 'as far as you know'?!" screeched Sebastian.

"Will you stop screaming!" said Zell. "You're giving me a headache. Nobody from the club has ever been hurt in a book."

"Except that one time with Mary Ann," said Frank.

"Pshaw!" said Zell. "That was her own darn fault."

"And when Clyde got an arrow to the butt."

Zell and Frank were distracted by their own laughter over their shared memory.

"Well, then I stand corrected," said Zell. "Nobody from the club has actually *died*. In *our* group anyhow. Don't know about historically speaking."

Sebastian resumed his show of fear by whimpering.

"Ugh. That odor is horrible," said Glo, wrinkling her nose.

"Yeah, the dead body stench," said Zell. "Can be pretty bad sometimes. Depends on how long it's been there."

"I thought they weren't real?" said Glo.

"Wellll," said Frank. "Not real-real. Just book real."

"So, what are we dealing with here?" asked Emiko, her finger tapping her chin. She was standing next to Zell looking down at the wire cage as if they were examining a footprint in the mud.

Forrest slowly inched up next to them. "Eww. He's naked."

"Brilliant observation," chuckled Zell.

"He's what!?" said Moonbeam as she tiptoed closer trying to get a look. "Goodness me! He's in a wire one-door trap!"

"What's that?" Glo asked.

"It's a humane animal trap," said Moonbeam. "Mostly used to capture destructive creatures like raccoons, foxes, bobcats, skunks, and beavers. We use them on our farm. Pests can get in, but they can't get out. Then you can stick the cage in your truck and relocate them out to the wilderness."

Zell crouched down and looked at the backside of the cage, where the man's face was located. "Looks like Randall Ward to me. Vee, can you bring your youthful eyesight over here? You got a look at him when he was yelling, didn't you?"

"Uh. Yeah. Okay." Vee went around to the back of the cage and leaned over. "Yeah. That's Randall Ward all right."

"Bingo!" said Frank. "We have our victim!"

I tried not to look, but I couldn't help myself. The man was indeed naked. He was scrunched so tightly into the wire cage that bubbles of his skin were pushed out through the holes.

"How in the world did a full-grown man get into this cage?" I asked. "He barely fits all scrunched up like that."

"A great leading question, Paige," said Emiko. She pulled her phone out of her pocket. "I'm writing down, 'how did man get in trap?'"

"Put down 'Why did he shoot at us,'" said Sebastian.

"Got it," said Emiko.

"Someone obviously put him in there. No way would he climb in there himself," said Moonbeam. "And my guess is that he was put in there either dead or passed out cold. Someone would have really had to jam him in there."

"Excellent point Moonbeam, my girl!" said Frank.

"It would take at least two people to make that happen," Emiko pointed out. "You'd have to kind of bend and fold him into it." She made folding gestures with her hands that made me cringe.

"More clues!" said Frank. "I like this group. Got some good heads in the game. We've had some bozos to work with in the past."

"Remember when that big dope Harold shot himself in the foot?" snickered Zell. "Had no business putting a gun in that guy's hand, that's for sure."

Sebastian gasped. "You said no club members got hurt! That's already the third person you mentioned."

"Was his own fault," grumbled Zell.

"Wait a minute," I said. "You told us we couldn't get hurt by Randall Ward's bullets. Now you're telling us a club member shot himself in the foot. So, which is it? We can get shot or we can't?"

"Geeze, woman," said Zell. "How am I supposed to know?"

"Hey, guys?" Emiko was still examining the trap. "Are those eggshells in there with him?"

Zell got closer. "Hmm. Looks like it. What do you think Vee? Frank?"

"There're eggshells on the ground over here, too," said Forrest. I noticed that he'd backed away from the cage and was hanging out near the side of the shed, scrolling on his phone. I didn't blame him for moving away. I did wonder if he had service, or if he was scrolling through pictures or something.

Sebastian went over to examine the shells. I think he was glad that no one asked him to inspect the body in the cage.

"Don't touch 'em!" said Zell. "First rule of book club, don't ever touch anything that could be evidence."

"Is that the first rule?" asked Frank. "I thought the first rule was don't tamper with the dead body."

"Who on earth is going to tamper with a dead body?" said Zell. "I think that one's a given."

The group clustered around the cage, and all agreed that it looked like colorful eggshells were scattered in the cage under and around the body. We walked over to Forrest and Sebastian and looked at the shell pieces near the shed.

"Looks like somebody's been getting in the hen house," said Frank.

"Real hens lay colorful eggs," said Moonbeam. "But they're subtle, pastel colors. These are much too vibrant and unnatural to be from hens. Why, they're almost florescent."

Sebastian picked up a stick and poked at the shells. Then he crouched down to get a better look. "You're right! These aren't from real eggs. They're those plastic two-part eggs they use for kids in Easter egg hunts. You know what I mean?"

The group agreed with Sebastian. They appeared to be broken pieces of fake plastic eggs.

"It's not Easter back at home. We need to find out if it's Easter time here," said Zell. "Our first clue!"

"As if the naked man in the wire animal trap isn't a clue," snickered Forrest.

"I heard that, young man. Bionic hearing, remember?" Zell tapped her ear. "But good for you. Correct. We'll call the eggs our second clue. Body in the trap is the first clue! Emiko, write that down."

"At home we'd be calling 911," I pointed out. "Do you think that's a thing here?"

"I'd give it a shot," said Zell. "Have no way of knowing if we're in current time or years past. I haven't seen much in this rural setting yet to indicate. The old junker cars he's got parked don't tell us the year, and his home is an old dump."

"And he has no clothes as a style giveaway," snorted Frank.

"So, we can be in any time? Like time travelers?" asked Emiko.

Zell hooted. "Never thought of it that way. But we're in whatever time the book is set. Could be anything at all since Miss Paige here read the first page before we read the blurb."

"Have you ever seen dinosaurs?" asked Forrest, giving away a glimpse of his youth.

"Nah. Not yet anyhow." Zell winked at him.

"Forrest, do you have service?" Glo asked.

"Yeah, five bars. How weird is that?"

"Not really weird," said Frank. "Just means that this one's set in modern times in a place with cell service."

Glo pulled out her phone and called the emergency number. She was told that a mounted officer was nearby and would be there soon. We were to stay at the scene until he arrived.

14

"Did you say a mounted officer – like on horseback?" asked Sebastian.

Glo nodded. "That's what the operator said."

"Oooo! This I want to see!" Sebastian blushed. "I saw mounted officers In New York City once ... patrolling during a parade. They are fab-u-lous!"

"They still have mounted officers in real life?" asked Emiko.

"Sure do, honey," said Moonbeam. "In big cities for crowd control and in parks. Especially in rural areas with lots of off-road places. Easier for horse-mounted police to get around."

"What an amazing job to have!" Emiko looked totally delighted with the concept.

"Oh, I remember you saying you ride?" Vee asked her.

"I do." Her face lit up. "It's my passion."

"What do you do for work?" asked Sebastian.

Emiko shifted from foot to foot and looked at the ground. "I'm an accountant. A CPA, to be precise."

"And looks like you hate every minute of it," Zell piped in, being unabashedly honest, of course.

Emiko took in a deep breath. "My parents were CPAs. It was always expected I'd do the same. Now that they're gone, I carried on the line. I'm brilliant with numbers." She said it with the same amount of enthusiasm a mother would say, 'I'm brilliant at changing diapers.'

"Speaking of which," said Zell, pointing. "He's comin' up behind you!"

We turned around to see an officer on horseback coming down the hill toward us. His horse was a magnificent glossy brown Quarter Horse. The man was riding with proud posture, as if born to the saddle. He was wearing a black cowboy hat with a police badge positioned front and center. He was clean-shaven, and his long dark hair flowed from under his cowboy hat. He looked relatively young for an officer but was built like a guy I wouldn't want to tussle with.

Glo came and stood next to me and whispered, "Emiko is looking at him the way you look at chocolate cheesecake."

I elbowed her in the ribs. "Glo! Shhh."

The officer rode up to a tree nearby and smoothly dismounted. He tied his horse, then approached the group. He tipped his hat. "Afternoon, folks. I'm officer Carter Sandoval."

We all stared at this imposing man; no one spoke.

"I understand ya'll found a dead body?"

Zell stepped forward with her usual bravado. "Yes, sir." She saluted him, and he smiled. "It's right this way." She walked back to the side of the shed. The officer followed her, and the rest of us trailed behind them.

"Um, hmm. Quite puzzling." He muttered. Then he took out his phone and snapped a series of photos. He pulled a small roll of yellow tape out of a pocket and strung it from the end of the shed, around branches of trees and bushes and to the opposite end of the shed.

"Have you touched anything, or moved anything, since you've arrived?"

"No, sir, Officer Sandoval, sir." Zell snapped to attention and saluted him again.

"You can call me Carter," he said. "I don't want anyone near the scene."

"Of course not, sir—Carter."

"Mind telling me what y'all are doing here?"

I felt panic rise in my chest. How on earth could we explain who we were or why we were standing in the man's yard?

"We're new to town," answered Zell. "We were taking a walk around the neighborhood. We stopped by to see if the neighbor who lived in this house was home, so we could say a proper hello. Then our cat got loose—"

Frank emitted a perfectly timed series of meows.

"—so we followed him to the back yard. Then he ran behind the shed. While we were searching for our cat—"

Frank meowed again and rubbed his head against Zell's leg.

"—we found this here body." Zell pointed to the body in the animal trap.

Carter smiled down kindly at the little lady and her cat.

We were all listening to Zell with rapt attention. I wasn't the only one shocked and impressed that they'd come up with this story on the fly. However, I quickly realized it appeared rehearsed. They'd probably used this story before. In other books. I closed my eyes and shook my head. Everything here was so utterly real it was impossible to retain the concept that these were characters. Of course, since we were trapped here until we solved the mystery, it was probably best if I thought of them as real people with potentially real bullets.

The officer used his radio to call in the finding, and requested a 'CSI tech.'

Glo leaned close and told me and Emiko, "That's a crime scene investigator technician."

"Thanks," said Emiko, continuing to keep an interested eye on Carter Sandoval.

"Can I have everyone over here, please?" said the officer. He walked away from the body to a clearing with some large rocks. "Take a seat if you wish." He pointed to the rocks. "You'll need to stay fifteen feet apart from each other, and no talking until I'm done taking statements."

"Do you have a tape measure?" asked Zell.

"You don't need to measure, ma'am. You can estimate. I'll need to speak with each of you, one at a time."

"Yes, sir!" said Zell.

"This is a small town, we're not so formal here. Y'all can call me Carter." He smiled down at Zell. I think he was grateful she didn't salute him again. "Who'd like to start us off?"

"Me first, Carter!" Sebastian called out, raising his hand and waving it in the air.

"Right this way."

Carter led Sebastian over to a set of old folding chairs on a deck behind the house. They took a seat, and we could see Sebastian gesturing wildly as he answered questions. I was glad we all paid attention to the lost cat story. From there, all we needed to do was report the facts.

Sebastian returned to the group. He was flushed with the excitement of giving his statement. "Whew! That was thrilling! He tapes your statement on his recorder, you know. Oh, he said someone else can go now."

Zell got up off the rock and marched over to give her statement.

"What did he ask you?" Glo whispered as Sebastian walked past her. "And keep your voice down."

"As you can imagine, he wanted to know how we came upon the body. Lost cat you know." He smirked, winked, and put his hands on his hips. He puffed out his chest. "Then he had me tell him what I saw. I told him about the body in the cage and the plastic egg pieces. I think he was riveted!"

"Most likely more by your presentation than the story," said Vee.

Sebastian took that as a compliment. "I've been told I do have a bit of a flair for the dramatic."

I looked at Glo and raised my eyebrows. She fake coughed and covered her mouth to hide her giggle.

We gave our statements one by one, then returned to our seats on the rocks. Finally, it was Emiko's turn. She was the last of the group. We watched her walk over to Carter.

Sebastian scooted over to a closer rock in the middle of the group. "Hmm. Look at that. He's watching her with a new level of interest. Oh, now look! The lingering hello-nice-to-meet-you handshake! His using the two-handed hold-and-pat, now. Comforting her after her traumatic experience. Ahh! Now he's pulling her chair closer to his."

"Sebastian! Stop that," said Moonbeam. Then she giggled. "A little harmless flirtation never hurt anyone."

"Flirtation?" Vee laughed.

"Sweetheart, I know these things. I'm a bit psychic, you know."

Forrest groaned and rolled his eyes.

Emiko completed her statement, which I noticed took quite a bit longer than ours, then she and Carter rejoined the group.

We stood around talking and waiting for the CSI tech to show up. Carter told us we could leave, but we were too invested in the outcome. We didn't tell him that, we just said we were curious. He told us to stay far out of the way and let the team do their work. It did end up being three people who were efficient and unemotional. We watched them inspect and photograph the scene. Sebastian felt proud to be able to point out the eggshells that were farther away from the cage, and they logged in that area, also. They finally loaded the entire cage with the man inside into the back of an aid car.

"We're all done here," said Carter. "I'll have all your statements typed up at the station. I need you to come by and verify and sign your statements. Today, please."

We all mumbled our agreement.

"And I don't want anybody leaving town."

Carter turned around, untied his horse, and rode off.

We all broke down into uncontrollable giggles.

15

"Well, good thing he told us not to leave town." Glo was still laughing at the officer's demand.

"Speaking of town," I said. "How are we going to get to the station? Do you think Glo's truck is here? But it won't seat all of us. Are there buses, you suppose?"

"Why don't we just take the van?" said Zell.

"What van?" I asked.

"The one at the inn, of course. How else do you think we get around?"

"But of course, the van," Glo said. She poked me in the arm, and we both shook our heads.

We walked back to the house, all talking about what we'd seen. Even though we knew we were in a murder mystery, it was deeply disturbing to actually see the victim.

"In a book the words are flat on the page, and your mind might conjure up an image," I said. "But to see it like that was—"

"The stuff of nightmares," said Vee.

"You get used to it," said Zell. "Just keep telling yourself, it's a character in a book. It's like watching a movie."

"A super creepy movie that you're living in," said Forrest.

"Exactly," I said. It was nice to see the teenager joining in our conversation. He was toning down his screen time and becoming more engaged. I guess seeing a dead body in a cage will do that to a person.

As soon as we got home, Glo and I went out and peeked into the garage. Sure enough, there was a big blue van parked there. It was large enough to hold eight people comfortably. How convenient.

"Can we grab dinner in town?" asked Vee.

"I vote yes!" said Zell. "It's one of the things I like best about these trips. Eating out at new restaurants."

"This is just a trip to you?" Sebastian looked at her like she had two heads.

"Not just a trip, young man. An adventure. An escapade. An experience! And a great chance to eat out at lots of different restaurants."

Sebastian pressed his fingers to his forehead and squinted his eyes shut.

Everyone went up to their rooms to change. We were all still in shock that everything we needed from our own homes was transported with us in those space-age bags, toothbrushes and all!

Glo and I were the first ones to come back down. We were sitting in the living room chatting as people started to join us.

Glo offered to drive to town. Since she was accustomed to her truck, the van would be no challenge for her. I called Theo to ask him where the police station was.

His laughter was so loud that the gang could hear him across the room. "Go north to downtown. You'll find it," he said.

From his response, and the farmlands that surrounded us, I figured we were in a very small town.

Emiko joined us dressed in what was clearly her CPA work clothes. Her pale blue suit and white blouse were plain but obviously of high quality. She looked a bit stiff, but lovely.

"I'm ready," said Frank, coming into the room and jumping up onto the sofa.

"Can we take a cat into town?" asked Sebastian, arriving in the living room just behind Frank. He'd dressed for our trip in crisply pressed slacks, a floral dress shirt, cornflower blue jacket, and a jaunty scarf. I tried not to stare, but it appeared that he was wearing mascara. Apparently, a trip to town meant it was time for him to pull out his formal attire.

"Can we take a cat to town!? My dear man," said Frank, "I am very experienced at book travel. You should be jumping for joy that I agree to join you."

"Oh, trust me, I am!" Sebastian said. "I just mean can we take a cat into the police station. And, like ... do you talk in front of everyone, or just us?"

"Don't know," said Frank, shrugging his shoulders.

"Don't know what?" asked Moonbeam, coming into the room in a bright red boho print maxi dress with a matching headband and carrying a reusable grocery bag as a purse. Her wild mane of brown and gray hair looked like it had a good brushing – which only succeeded in making it frizzier.

"Don't know if I can talk in this book," said Frank. "Sometimes I can, sometimes I can't. If I can talk to others, we immediately know it's a paranormal mystery. Expands the possibilities of the story."

~ ~ ~

Glo drove slowly through the countryside. We

were in the most beautiful area. It even outshined my glorious home state of Colorado. The colors were more vivid than in the natural world. The skies were a dazzling, brilliant blue. The trees and grass were in shades of green, each one more vibrant than the last. The snow-topped mountains were taller than any I'd ever seen, the sun a more golden yellow. It was like driving in a postcard that had been photoshopped to enhance its beauty.

"Is it always like this, Zell?" I asked her, as we all ohhed and ahhed over the scenery.

"Nah. It depends on the book. It's like this when an author likes adjectives. Sometimes the setting is kind of bland, and sometimes things don't quite measure up."

"What do you mean?" asked Glo.

"You might have a lake in the backyard, but later it turns into a stream. Or you leave the house in the morning, but the next scene occurs at night. It's like the author goofed and you're stuck with it."

"That's dope," said Forrest.

"Dope?" said Zell. "I thought dope meant marijuana. You know, like Cheech and Chong called it."

Forrest stared at her, confused.

I laughed. "That was in the seventies, Zell. Dope means awesome."

"Huh. Well then. This trip is dope," said Zell, nodding her head.

Vee snorted. "It's kind of reserved for teenagers."

"I'm doping eighty years old. I can do what I want," she sniffed.

"We're here!" said Moonbeam. "Time to meet the fuzz."

We all laughed as we got out of the van and headed into the police station.

I hadn't really thought of how incongruent our group was until I spotted a few of the workers glancing at us sideways. There we were. A tiny eighty-year-old overly-confident senior citizen leading the pack. A brooding teenager, a tattooed biker chick, a flamboyantly dressed gay man, a fifty-year-old hippie, a petite Asian CPA in business attire, a Siamese cat ... and me and Glo.

"Are you all together?" asked the desk clerk with a confused glance at our motley group.

"We are," said Zell. "We're here following official orders. Officer Carter Sandoval has requested that we review and approve our statements as witnesses in the discovery of "—she leaned across the desk to get closer to the clerk— "a dead body."

The clerk's eye's widened and she swallowed. "One moment, please." She scuttled off down the hall, I assumed to check out the story.

Zell turned to the group and clapped her hands. "Let's be quick about this folks. I saw a pizza place just down the road as we pulled in. Looks like a good choice, and I am hungry."

The clerk returned. "We'll need each of you to come back separately."

"Does the cat get to make a statement, too?" Frank asked.

The clerk looked directly at Frank. "I'm afraid not. Humans only when it's a human death."

We all turned toward the clerk, our mouths hanging open.

Sebastian whispered the word we were all thinking, "Paranormal."

The clerk looked down at her clipboard. "Can we start with Lucille Lowenstein?"

"We don't have anyone by that—"

"Right here!" said Moonbeam, raising her hand and moving to the front of the group. She began to follow the clerk but turned around and gave us a saucy wink on the way out.

By the time we'd all approved and signed our statements, we were hungry and eager to check out the pizza place that Zell had mentioned. We opted to walk the short distance; everyone was in awe over the charming small town and anxious to see more.

"The town isn't all that different from Cascade Valley," said Glo. "Real typical small town. Lots of the same types of shops and businesses."

"It's hard to believe this is all fictional," I said.

"I know," agreed Emiko. "I'm finding it difficult to wrap my head around that. It's not logical."

"And you do have that logical brain!" said Sebastian.

Frank nodded his head from his comfortable position in Sebastian's arms. "Logic will be necessary."

We funneled into the restaurant and took the largest table in the back of the room. After much deliberation, we ordered four different pies plus cheesy garlic breadsticks. The waitress asked Frank if he'd like anchovies, and he requested a double serving. She wrote it down as if a cat hadn't just made the order.

"I'm beginning to see the validity of Zell's fixation on checking out the local restaurants," said Glo. "Crime-solving is tiring work. I'm starved!"

Forrest held up a newspaper. "I lifted a local paper from the kiosk out front."

"Nice job, Forrest," said Moonbeam. "It wasn't lifted though, honey, those are free."

"Whatever." He placed the paper on the table in

front of his mother.

The server brought the pizzas to the table and there was a frenzy of slice distribution. At last, everyone was eating and looking pretty darn happy about it.

Moonbeam unfolded the paper and glanced at the date. “It’s June. So not Easter season.”

“That for sure makes those Easter eggs a clue, right?” said Forrest around a mouthful.

“Indeed it does!” said Zell. “You’re like a regular Sherlock Holmes!”

Forrest smiled proudly, but then took another big bite of pizza to cover it up.

Moonbeam returned to perusing the paper. “The whole town is planning their Changing Season Festival. So must be like welcoming the summer. It looks like a big deal. Happens not far from where our house is situated in a big section of acreage owned by the city.”

“Ohh! I hope we’re still here for that,” said Zell. “I love festivals.”

“Aha!” said Moonbeam. “Here’s something being discussed in several letters to the editor. It’s about Randall Ward. Apparently, he was an anti-social recluse. He rarely left his property.”

“He did look like that kind of person,” said Emiko. “And his property reflected that, as well.”

“Listen to this! He was dumping all his waste in the river, creating an ongoing flow of pollution. He’s already been fined for it but hadn’t stopped his actions. There’s a petition going around town that was calling for him to be arrested and charged under terms of the US EPA – that’s the United States Environmental Protection Agency. If that happened, he could have faced a fine up to twenty-five hundred dollars per day plus a year in jail and be required to remedy the situation. There’s a lot of angry people who are talking about the petition."

Frank's head jerked up from his big plate of anchovies. "Suspects!" he shouted, spewing bits of fish all over the table.

16

"Definitely! They're our suspects!" agreed Sebastian, bouncing excitedly in his seat.

Zell put her finger up to her mouth in the universal sign for quiet. She looked left and right. "This isn't the place to discuss our business," she said. "You never know who's listening. Let's talk about this at home after we pick up some dessert from the bakery next door."

Leave it to Zell to spot the bakery. She really took her job of visiting local food establishments seriously.

We finished up our pizza and reconvened at the bakery next door. This wasn't a quick stop, given that every person in the group had to completely inspect the vast array of choices in the glass case. Every item looked mouthwateringly delicious.

A woman with a shock of dazzling blue hair and an apron to match came out of the back room wiping her hands on a towel. "Welcome to Birdie's Bakery! My goodness, where did everyone come from? The shop was empty a moment ago!"

"We're all together," I explained.

"None of you look familiar," she said, glancing around at everyone.

"We're new in town. Visitors," said Glo.

"Oh, how nice! I'm Birdie. Nice to meet y'all." Her smile faded when she saw Frank. "Oh dear. You've brought a cat with you."

"He's very well-behaved," said Glo, to which Frank made gagging noises.

Glo picked him up and tucked him in to her arms.

"He'll be perfectly quiet, and I'll keep him in my arms. Would that be okay with you?" she asked.

"I suppose," said Birdie, but she didn't really look comfortable with a cat in her bakery.

I heard Glo whispering to Frank, and his muffled grunts in reply.

A group of four children came tumbling into the shop, saying "Hi, Mom" to Birdie. We could have guessed they were related. They all had the same bright blue hair as their mother.

"Why would you dye your kids' hair blue?" whispered Emiko.

"I think it's cool," said Vee, with a shrug.

Birdie came around and gave each of the kids a quick hug. "Y'all sit right here and start your homework while I take care of these customers." She glanced back at us. "It's almost summer vacation, but they need to finish up the year. Hard to focus when the weather's so nice. I have the kids come here so I can keep an eye on them."

The brood seemed well behaved, and they were most likely familiar with the routine in their mother's bakery. They answered her politely, sat at one of the tables, and began taking work out of their backpacks.

"Now, we ought to start with some samples. I'll be just a sec!" She bustled into the back room.

Birdie returned with a massive tray filled with miniature paper muffin cups. "I call these 'Birdie's Bits'," she said with a grin. "It's all the crumbly parts from the cookie sheets and whatnot. They're all labeled. Gives you a nice taste of things. And waste not, want not!" She put the tray on the counter, and everyone reached for the samples.

Zell was the first to order, and she wasn't shy. She bought four different treats, then began chatting with the woman while her items were boxed up.

"So, did you hear about Randall Ward turning up dead?" She sounded like a gossipy local, which did exactly what she set out to do, I was sure. Birdie opened right up.

"Isn't that something!" gasped the blue-haired woman. "It's all anyone can talk about today. It doesn't surprise me, though. He was awful. A destroyer of the environment and he didn't care one lick about what he was doing. Made lots of people pretty darn angry."

"I bet!" said Zell, leaning forward and giving Birdie her full attention. "So, who'd he tick off?"

"Who didn't he tick off!? First, all the farmers and ranchers who use water from the river, of course. It affects their property even if it's down a ways."

"Ohhh. That's awful." Moonbeam had been standing near the ladies and she added her two cents. "I'm sure it has an effect on their use of the water for animals and crops," she said. "And to have someone in your community who is so insensitive to environmental issues." She shook her wild mane of hair, clearly upset on their behalf.

"Well, thank you, ma'am!" said Birdie, inclining her head at Moonbeam respectfully while she packed up more of our pastries. "You clearly understand the situation. Plus, can you imagine? All the parents whose kids swim in that river! And the folks who like to fish!" She was really revved up now that she was on the topic.

"That man didn't leave his property, except to grumble his way through the grocery once a week. And he didn't pay for garbage service! Plus, I heard his old septic system probably had leaks. So, what does that tell you? Where did all his waste go? The river! He was a danger to us all."

Moonbeam nodded. "I bet the whole community was up in arms."

"You got it! That's why they have that petition going. Well. Had it going, I guess. Now that he's gone, the town can go in and clean up all his junk."

"He doesn't have any wife or kids?" asked Zell, once again fishing for information.

"He did have a wife. She left. Probably tired of the mess. And a couple of kids that she took with her. But that was like twenty years ago."

The bell on the door jingled and a few new customers walked in. Birdie packaged up the rest of our purchases, gave us a happy good-bye, and turned her attention to the newcomers.

17

The energy level in our library was off the charts. The group wasn't just buzzing from the sugar in all the bakery items we were noshing on, but from the information we'd gathered in town. It seemed like we were well on our way to figuring out this mystery and getting out of this book.

"We usually appoint a note-taker," said Zell.

Emiko raised her hand. Zell pointed at her. "Thank you, Emiko."

Emiko pulled out her phone and sat poised, ready to capture our discussion.

"Now we need a group meeting leader."

"That's not you?" asked Sebastian.

"Heavens, no!" Zell said. "I step in when I must, but goodness it gets tiring. I'd rather be part of the peanut gallery, thank you very much."

"I'm happy to do it," I offered.

There was a smattering of applause. I held back my laughter over the ridiculous situation I'd found myself in. I figured if I led the discussion, perhaps I could keep the group on track, and we'd efficiently dissect the mystery. Then we could get out of here sooner.

"Don't you need the murder board?" asked Zell.

"I thought it was called an evidence board," said Vee.

"I've heard it called a murder *map*," said Moonbeam.

"I thought it was a suspect board, or a detective board," added Emiko. "I saw that in a Hallmark mystery movie."

I could see that this group was going to be the opposite of efficient. I took a deep breath. "Whatever it's called. Where do you suppose I'd find it?" I asked.

"I'll show her," said Frank in that annoyed tone of voice mothers use when their children can't find something. He got up slowly and groaned, as if it were a great effort.

I followed Frank to a closet door on the far wall. I opened it to a large rolling whiteboard. There were two new unopened boxes of markers on the ledge.

"Well, isn't this convenient." I rolled the whiteboard out in front of the group.

"Note that it's double-sided," said Zell. "Side one is for the suspects." She held up one finger, then she held up a second. "Side two is for notes and our to-do list and whatever. Though I suggest writing it down on paper, too, since *someone*" — she looked sideways at Frank— "occasionally erases important data."

"Once!" said Frank. "I did that one time."

"Three times," said Zell.

"Zelda, honestly!" said Frank in a huff. "Three little times and I'm branded as a board-wiper. Geesh."

"I don't think that—"

"Shall we get started?" I asked in a loud voice, interrupting their squabble. "In order to begin listing suspects we need to have some. How do we find out who organized the petition against Randall Ward, and names of people who have already signed it?"

"I know a bit about petitions," said Moonbeam, leaning forward in her chair.

That brought smiles from the group. She did seem like the kind of person who would know how to influence change through grassroots methods.

"The article doesn't say what stage the petition is in, but it appears that it hasn't been filed yet. The initiators are likely still in the process of collecting signatures. This is most effective when done in person. Like when you see people in public parks, malls, or outside of grocery stores with clipboards, you know? The question is, how do we find out who initiated the petition, and how do we get the names of the signers?"

"I can handle that," said Emiko.

"You can?" said Vee.

"Sure. I'm somewhat of an online research savant. I sometimes help a local investigator friend of mine. It's a hobby."

"So then, let me get this straight. You ride horses, do your CPAing, and tinker in online investigations?" Vee laughed. "I like you more every day, girl."

Emiko blushed at the compliment. "Just trying to be helpful."

"Great! Do you have a computer in your room?" I asked her.

"I do. And I'm already hooked up to the house internet."

"How'd you do that?" asked Glo.

"Savant," said Frank, with a knowing nod.

Sebastian waved a piece of paper in the air. "Notes!"

"Yes, great idea, Sebastian. Can you start us off by reviewing what's on the notes?"

"Certainly." He looked proud to be called upon. He unfolded the paper, cleared his throat, and began. "According to the club notes, we need to first talk to the locals."

"We've begun that one!" said Moonbeam.

"And we need to explore the area."

"Perhaps that can be our goal for tomorrow?" said Emiko.

I opened the box of markers and started to write the list on the board.

1 – Talk to the locals.
2 – Explore the area.

"We are supposed to figure out who to trust and who to avoid. Then make a list of suspects and discover alibis, determine motive and opportunity, and detect lies." I added these items to the list.

3 – Who to trust? Who to avoid?
4 – Alibis, motive, opportunity.
5 – Determine who is lying.

"That looks good, Paige," said Glo.

"These aren't set in stone, you know," said Frank. "Each book is different, and some books don't follow that plotline. And most authors love to throw in a bunch of red herrings. Everybody listen up!" He tapped his curled paw on a chair, suddenly sounding like a small, furry general, but with a marshmallow soft fist. "We must stay loose and be willing to pivot if necessary."

"Do you all agree that we should explore the neighborhood tomorrow?" I asked the group. "See who lives and works along the river. The people who would most be affected by the pollution."

Everyone thought that was a good idea.

"We can also talk to some locals that way. We might get some tips," pointed out Forrest. He'd been so quiet I nearly forgot he was in the room. But I supposed with this group it was hard to get a word in edgewise.

I could see that everyone was getting tired. It had been a very long and crazy day. "What do you think? Is this enough for today?" I asked.

There was a chorus of voices saying "Yeah."

"If we're done, you're supposed to say, 'meeting

adjourned,'" said Frank.

"Since when?" said Zell, her face scrunched up.

"It makes sense. Otherwise, how will we know if the meeting is over?"

"Frankie, we know the meeting is over because Paige just said, 'Is this enough for today?' and everyone said yeah."

"So, then why can't she say, 'meeting adjourned'?" Frank persisted.

I tapped a marker on the board. "Meeting adjourned!"

~ ~ ~

Everyone plodded up the two flights of stairs as if climbing a mountain. They all looked as exhausted as I felt. Some wandered into the kitchen for a bedtime snack, others aimed right for the third flight of stairs to the bedrooms. Those tired folks called out good night in sleepy voices.

I would have loved a cup of chamomile tea, but I had enough conversation for the day, so instead went directly up to my room. I washed up, brushed my teeth, and changed into an oversized t-shirt and shorts for sleeping. I grabbed a book, fluffed my pillows, and climbed into bed. Two minutes later there was a soft knock at my door. I groaned and got back out of bed.

"Glo! You brought tea!"

"Of course I did, silly girl. I know you like a cup before bed, but figured you were avoiding the uhh, peanut gallery, as Zell would say."

We both laughed at that. She carried in the tray with two cups and a pot of tea on it, and I shut the door behind her.

Glo went about preparing the tea while she chattered. "Isn't this the most insane thing ever to happen to anyone ... ever?! I mean, seriously! We're in a *book*! There was a dead man in an animal trap! A *naked* dead man who had tried to shoot us! And the house came along with us and brought all our stuff along with it!"

She took a breath and I added, "Let's not forget Frank — a talking cat with a Napoleon complex."

Glo covered her mouth as she let out a peal of laughter. "Oh, man!" she sputtered. "Frank and Zell together are a riot!"

Once our laughter subsided, we took our teacups to the bed and sat beside each other, leaning on the headboard.

"Can you believe that GeeGee used to do this?" I asked. "Go into books and solve mysteries?"

"It boggles the mind," said Glo. "I bet she's laughing now, watching the two of us."

We were suddenly quiet, thinking of the woman we thought we knew, but who carried a massively big secret.

"I can sure see why she didn't leave the house to my mother," I said. "Mom would lose her mind over this."

"Well, I'm kind of losing mine," laughed Glo.

"But you're always a little cray-cray."

She looked at me with an exaggerated expression of horror, pretending to be offended. Then she smirked. "Yeah, yeah, okay. Guilty as charged. But this is a bit out of your wheelhouse."

"When you told me to try something new, I was thinking more like yoga classes and trying out some vegetarian recipes. Nowhere in your box of birthday gifts was a magical mystery book club."

"You did do yoga with Moonbeam, Zell, and Sebastian."

We pictured that scene and we both laughed. Glo snorted tea out her nose, which got us revved up again. We released all our pent-up emotions laughing until tears ran down our faces.

18

"It's like herding cats!" I complained.

"Hey!" said Frank.

I raised my eyebrows at him.

He chuckled. "I resemble that remark."

"Surprisingly, the cat is the one ready to go," said Glo.

We were standing on the porch waiting for the rest of the group to come out. There were several last-minute bathroom runs (Moonbeam and Emiko) — an "I forgot my sweater" (Zell) — an "I can't possibly wear these jeans, they have a smudge" (Sebastian) — and one "I need to get my charger" (Forrest). Where Vee was, I had no idea.

At long last we were all gathered and headed down the road for a neighborhood walk to investigate the homes along the river. One might have thought we were going on a day hike instead of a stroll down the street based on the Moonbeam's backpack and Zell's trekking poles. We had decided to start with the apple orchard located between us and Randall Ward's property. It appeared to be important since we'd landed there on our first day.

The home on the orchard property was a well-maintained, laid-back ranch style. There were three teenage girls hanging out on the front porch. I stifled a giggle when I noticed Forrest peek over his phone to clandestinely check out the girls.

"Will they think it's weird that we just materialized next door?" I asked Zell.

"Nah. We'd have been written into the story.

We're always where we're s'posed to be. Then we're written out when we're done. Moved away or something. It's a clever system."

"Interesting," said Glo, tapping her chin.

"Hi there!" called out Moonbeam, waving at the girls. "We're the new folks from next door."

We stopped on the street in front of the house.

"Hiya!" called out an energetic, willowy redhead as she jumped deftly down over the last three deck stairs.

The other two girls joined her, coming down off the porch to greet us. I was shocked that teenagers would be so hospitable. But I guessed that was small town living for you.

"I'm Duchess. This is my house." She pointed to the cute girl next to her with long wheat-colored hair. "This is Brandy."

"Hi ya'll!" said Brandy.

"And this is Selena."

"Hi!" The tall, slender Black girl with gorgeous, shiny, long hair bestowed us with a brilliant smile. "Welcome to the neighborhood."

The three of them came to stand in front of us. They looked like a cross between cheerleaders and basketball players with their glowing beauty and their tall height and long limbs. I thought Forrest was going to spontaneously combust.

"Looks like you have an apple orchard back there," said Zell, looking past them toward the property behind the home.

"Sure do! Three different varieties," said Duchess. "Y'all want to see it?"

"We'd love to!" was said in unison by me, Glo, Zell, and Moonbeam. Then we chuckled uncomfortably. I thought it might be wise if we toned down our enthusiasm, but the girls seemed to overlook it.

Brandy pointed over toward Randall Ward's house. "Did y'all hear that the guy next door was found dead in a box?"

"A wire animal trap," said Zell.

I glanced sideways at her, not sure if she should be volunteering facts that showed our involvement.

"We found the dead guy," said Zell.

So much for my concern.

The girls' eyes all got wide, their brows rising on their foreheads.

"Seriously?" said Brandy.

"That must have been sooo creepy," added Selena.

"Yeah, it was," said Glo. "Did you know him at all?"

"Not really," said Brandy. "He wasn't a friendly sort. And you know he was polluting the river. We never talked to him because my parents hated him for that."

"Did they, now?" said Zell.

"Do you live nearby?" asked Moonbeam.

"Kinda. But my parents manage the orchard and the stables here. We could go meet them. They're repairing some fencing down by the river."

We followed the girls through the orchard where they invited us to each pick an apple to taste. They were fresh and crisp. I noticed that the girls were anxious to show Forrest the different varieties. He was juggling three apples in his hands and had a goofy smile on his face.

"These are amazing!" Moonbeam gushed. "You couldn't find anything like these in a store."

I whispered to Glo, "There shouldn't even be ripe apples in June."

Zell heard me and whispered back, "Apparently the author of this book didn't know that."

We walked through the stand of trees and past the old barn where we'd hidden from Randall Ward's bullets. I shivered from the memory. Just past that old barn was a newer, larger barn that was home to several horses. Beyond that was a corral.

"You have horses!" sighed Emiko.

"Do you ride?" asked Selena.

"Yes, I do! Wow, you have some beauties. Is that one a Tennessee Walker?"

"Sure is," said Duchess. "You should come over and ride sometime."

"Could I really? Oh, my gosh! That would be awesome. Thanks."

"There's my parents," said Brandy, pointing.

"Howdy," said the woman approaching us with a friendly smile. She looked exactly like an older version of Brandy.

"Good day," said Brandy's father, a tall, lanky but muscular man with a cowboy hat and a long black braid going down his back. He clearly had passed on the genes for Brandy's height and build.

"Mr. and Mrs. Swiftwater, these are our new neighbors," said Duchess. "Oh, gosh. I'm sorry. I don't know any of your names."

"I'm Paige," I said holding out my hand to shake.

"Cheyenne Swiftwater, and this is my husband, Outlaw."

"Outlaw?" said Zell, as usual lacking any filters. "Is that your real name or a nickname?"

He laughed. "You sure get right to the point, don't cha, little lady? Would be a nickname."

"I have one, too; my full name's Zelda, but you

can call me Zell."

One by one we introduced ourselves.

"These are the people who found Mr. Ward's body," said Duchess.

"Oh, my goodness!" said Cheyenne. "That must have been horrifying!" Her hands flew to her face.

"It was pretty ugly," said Zell, wrinkling her face. Then, she went full steam ahead. "I don't want to speak ill of the dead, but I heard people around here hated the guy."

I was shocked at her candor, but I noticed that both Cheyenne and Outlaw stiffened, their faces giving away their feelings about their neighbor.

"That'd be true," said Outlaw. "He had no regard for the land. Used the river as his personal dumping ground. Was a constant battle. We have to take regular readings of the wells to be sure the water isn't tainted. And this here barbed wire fence." He motioned to the fence they'd been repairing. "It's necessary so the horses don't get into the garbage that's always floating by."

"I can't say I'm sad to see him go. It was a rightful end—" started Cheyenne, but Outlaw put his hand on her arm, and she stopped talking.

Duchess called out, "Hey, Dad!"

I glanced at Emiko who suddenly blushed a brilliant rosy hue. I turned around to see Duchess's father strolling across the property. It was Officer Carter Sandoval – the man who responded to our "there's a dead man in a cage" emergency call.

"Well, if y'all don't look familiar," he said.

"They're our new neighbors," said Duchess.

"You don't say," said Carter with a smirk.

"Oh! You must have met them when you got the

call next door!" said Selena. "They said they're the ones who found him."

"That's right, girls. I've already met our new neighbors." His eyes traveled over the group of us.

"We've been showing them around the property," said Duchess.

"Good job. Now y'all run along. I got it from here."

"Thanks, Dad!"

"Thanks, Mr. Sandoval," said Selena and Brandy.

Carter turned to us with his hands on his hips, looking just a bit imposing. "What brings you to my place?" he asked.

"We're out meeting all the neighbors!" said Moonbeam with a sparkle in her eye. It was hard to see anything but honesty and joy in her face.

"Is the Missus at home?" asked Zell, once again lacking any filters.

"No Missus. Just me and Duchess," he said.

Moonbeam poked Emiko in the arm and winked.

Glo tipped her head at me, and we moved Moonbeam away from the group. Glo spoke quietly to her. "Moonbeam, stop encouraging ideas of romance," she admonished her. "We're here to solve a mystery."

Moonbeam looked crestfallen. "You're right. I tend to get carried away."

I put my hand on her shoulder. "It's okay. We just need to keep our eye on the goal. Remember, none of this is real, and we need solve this mystery and get out of here as soon as we can."

19

As soon as we left Carter's house, I put up my hand to get everyone's attention. I wanted to prevent any discussion from occurring out in public. "We'll chat about this later, at the inn."

"Chat?" said Moonbeam, looking confused. Then it hit her. "Ohhh, right. Chat. Like a debriefing..."

"Shh." I put my finger to my lips. "Does anyone know where Frank went?" I asked.

"You know cats," said Zell. "Always slinking off somewhere. I'm sure he'll catch up when he's good and ready. Can't tell that boy what to do, that's for sure."

"I thought he was a man," said Forrest.

There was a round of giggling.

We walked down the street and quickened our pace when we passed Randall Ward's property. None of us were interested in revisiting the sight of that horrible scene.

The home that was just past his property was a gorgeous contemporary log cabin. It was beautifully maintained, and the landscaping was lush and tasteful. We stopped to admire the home, and of course, to see if anyone was there.

There was a loud bang that came from the backyard.

"That was a gunshot!" yelled Vee, running toward the sound.

"Vee! Get back here!" Sebastian shouted.

"Why are you running *toward* the gun?" Moonbeam yelled in the loudest non-Moonbeam voice I'd ever heard from her.

"We can't let her go alone!" hollered Emiko, running after Vee.

"We need to see what's happening!" yelled Glo, running after them.

"No! Glo! What are you doing?" I ran after her.

"I'm going too!" yelled Forrest, and I could hear him directly behind me.

"Don't leave us here!" I glanced back as I ran to see Sebastian, Zell, and Moonbeam taking up the rear.

We ran through a large property filled with lush, raised garden beds and a small orchard of fruit trees.

Just beyond the fruit trees, Vee, Emiko and Glo abruptly stopped running and I nearly ran into them. Sebastian did run into me, almost knocking both of us to the ground. Zell and Moonbeam were panting in their efforts to catch up with us.

We froze. In front of us stood a small woman aiming a pistol at a large target that was adhered to the front of a stack of hay bales. The bales were lined up near the riverbank. She shot again and nearly hit the center bullseye.

A familiar man's voice called out from our right, "Nice shot, Daisy!"

"Frank?!" I didn't mean to yell his name, but it slipped out. The woman – Daisy – turned around and spotted us.

"Hello there! You must be Frank's friends!" She set her pistol down and approached us. "I'm Daisy Remlinger. Glad to get a chance to meet all my new neighbors."

Frank jumped down off the tree stump he'd been sitting on. "Told ya they're a fun bunch of folks." He came to stand next to Daisy and she crouched down to pet him.

We made the round of introductions, then Daisy invited us in to meet her husband. "I just made a fresh batch of cider. I get the apples from Carter," she said. "I hear you've already met him when you found that smelly old skunk's body in the trap."

"Wow. Sounds like you weren't friends with your neighbor," said Zell.

"That's an understatement," Daisy scowled. "Ward was a stinky, dirty mess. He dumped all his waste in the river causing a real problem for us." She gestured to her gardens. "Contaminated water can destroy our crops. Our apple trees are already suffering since our wells can't keep up. We have to test them every day as it's just a matter of time before they'll be tainted, too. Bless Carter for sharing his crop of apples with us this year."

She shook her head. "Enough talk of that nasty man. Good riddance, I say. Come on in."

I glanced at Glo and we both raised our eyebrows in silent communication.

Daisy opened the door to her home and gestured us inside.

"Oh, my!" Moonbeam spread her arms to sweep the large open space. The interior of the home reflected the log cabin vibe. The walls were rustic knotty pine and blended perfectly with the stone fireplace. Large windows let in an abundance of natural light. Live plants decorated nearly every corner. Warm woven rugs adorned the plank wood floors, and comfortable-looking furniture encircled the fireplace. A wood dining table lined with benches sat beneath a chandelier made of deer antlers. Several matching antler lamps sat on end tables. The overall vibe was natural and cozy.

"Your home is absolutely glorious!" gushed Glo. We all made sounds of agreement.

"Thank you," said Daisy. "We love it here. Let me go get my husband." She turned and went down a hallway.

"Frank! How did you get here?" I asked.

"Uhh. Walked. On my perfectly usable four limbs," he replied, holding up a front leg and wiggling it in my direction.

"I mean, you've already made friends with the neighbor? Like in the last hour? When we were talking to Carter?"

"I'm a friendly sort of guy," he said, shrugging his shoulders in a very human-like motion. "People love cats, you know."

"I sure hope she didn't shoot the deer to get all those antlers!" said Moonbeam, pointing at the chandelier and the lamps.

"Oh, my heavens, no!" gasped Daisy, returning to the room with a tall, slender man behind her. "Those are all shed naturally.

"This is my husband, Jeremiah. Honey, these are our new neighbors. They live in that new inn on the other side of Carter's place."

"Mornin'," he said, reaching up to tip his hat just like a real cowboy. I'd become used to that gesture in the rural areas of Colorado. He wasn't wearing a hat indoors, thought, so the gesture was a pantomime of the real thing.

Daisy made the introductions, as we reminded her of our names. There was quite a large group of us, so I didn't blame her for not remembering. I was the same way with new people. I'd get distracted by the conversation and within minutes forget everyone's names.

"Can I get y'all some apple cider?" asked Daisy.

We all welcomed a taste and she stepped off to the kitchen, leaving us in the living room with Jeremiah.

"Grab a seat, folks." He took his own place on a

wooden rocking chair near the fireplace.

"This coffee table is amazing!" said Forrest, examining the table base made from a tree branch.

"Made it myself," said Jeremiah. "From a fallen branch."

"It's so cool," said Forrest.

"Ever done any woodworking?"

"Nah." Forrest shook his head.

"I could show you how to make one of these," said Jeremiah. "I got lots of equipment in my barn."

"Oh, man! That would be dope," said Forrest.

I glanced at Moonbeam and noticed her somber expression. I'm sure she was thinking that it was nice to see her teen son so engaged, but that we wouldn't be here long enough for Forrest to get a woodworking lesson.

"What do you think about your neighbor's horrible demise?" Zell asked. Of the group of us she was the only one who stayed focused on the murder mystery. The rest of us were enthralled by the people – um, characters – and the setting.

Jeremiah's face turned hard. "Serves him right," he growled. "The local wildlife depends on that river. He was a self-centered old fool who didn't give a hoot about anything. We've been after him since he moved in to dispose of his waste properly, but he shut us out. Now, finally! We can clean up his property and return the area to its natural state. We plan to—"

"Here you go, fresh apple cider! You're going to love this, I made it this morning. I warmed it up and added some cinnamon sticks." She glanced sideways at her husband, and I caught a slight shake of her head.

Darn it all! Daisy's enthusiastic voice was loud enough to drown out the rest of Jeremiah's rant that faded off into an uncomfortable grimace. It seemed they were keeping each other in check so they wouldn't say too much.

Daisy guided the pleasant conversation during the remainder of our visit. Jeremiah quietly sipped his cider and listened.

~ ~ ~

On our walk home I brought up what I presumed we were all thinking. "It appears that all our neighbors are suspects."

"Daisy can't be a suspect!" said Moonbeam. "She's much too nice and friendly. She invited us into her home!"

"And not Carter," said Emiko, with a slight blush and a tilt of her head. Moonbeam looked at her with a smirk and a smile.

"I mean ... because he's the local law officer!" Emiko stammered. "The police don't go around killing people and shoving them into wire traps!"

"Police officers aren't all good guys, you know," said Vee with a sour expression.

That led me to remember that Vee was with us by court order, which could affect her opinion.

"Cheyenne and Outlaw are such kind people," said Glo. "And they have a lovely, polite daughter. I liked them."

Frank cleared his throat to get our attention. We looked down to where he was trotting along next to us.

"Just cuz you met 'em and you like 'em doesn't mean they're innocent."

20

We returned to the inn just after noon. The group decided we should head back into town to see what we could learn about the local people.

"What do you say we have lunch at a restaurant?" Zell suggested.

"Ah, right. Your main priority," laughed Sebastian. "I'm in."

Everyone liked the idea. There was a flurry of activity while people used the restrooms, gathered up sweaters and purses, and then we once again gathered in the living room ready to leave.

"I say we find ourselves a good Mexican restaurant," said Zell. "I have a hankering for chips and salsa."

"Do you ever not have a hankering for chips and salsa?" asked Frank.

"Ah, you know me so well, my little furry friend. Is that a yes?" She looked around at all of us with wide eyes and her little octogenarian face.

We had no choice. We all agreed to Zell's idea and piled into the van to return to downtown. During the drive there was plenty of sightseeing chatter.

"The author of this book sure likes to describe the setting," said Zell, pointing out the charming, sunshiny downtown filled with adorable shops and happy people.

I looked at Glo and our eyes met. I knew what she was thinking, same as me. *Was this really happening?*

Cheerful people waved and smiled when we stopped to allow them to cross the street. Most of them had dogs or children. It was Hallmark at its best. Well, except for the murder. A naked dead man in a cage didn't fit the scene at all.

There were a variety of restaurants to choose from, including a fun-looking Mexican choice. Glo parked along the street not far from it. We tumbled out of the van and made our way to the restaurant. Hanging baskets of flowers were everywhere along the street, and shops were colorful and inviting. The streets were as clean as Disneyland, the capital of tidy roadways.

We stepped into a colorful restaurant with authentic decorations and music. We found a large round table that fit our group. The server brought several baskets of chips and trays with an assortment of different salsas. Zell was happily tasting one the moment the server set them down. We perused the menus, and the server took our orders. It took longer than necessary as everyone seemed to take their decision making very seriously and had far too many questions about the options. The server seemed surprisingly cheerful about that, and I chalked it up to small town charm.

"Good afternoon, folks," said a deep voice from behind me.

I spun around. "Carter! Hello."

"I see you found our favorite Mexican restaurant."

"Isn't it the only one?" asked Frank, twitching his ears.

Carter laughed. "Yep. And lucky to say, it's mighty good. I hear you've been making the rounds of the neighborhood. Hope you're just being friendly and not stepping into a murder investigation."

Emiko was blushing furiously and stammered, "No! No, we aren't. Just meeting people. Getting to know the town. We're new, you know, so—"

Glo put her hand on Emiko's arm, and she snapped her mouth closed.

"That's good. We don't want our citizens involved in a police investigation."

"So, you've determined that it's a murder?" asked Zell, munching another chip.

Carter nodded, then stopped the motion abruptly. "As I said, we keep our citizens safe by handling investigations at the professional level. Enjoy your lunch, folks."

As soon as Carter left, I spoke up quickly before anyone could bring up our neighbors. "Let's save all our opinions for our book club meeting later at the inn. We should decide how we're going to ... umm ... *get to know the town*."

"We could walk a circular route from here," said Vee.

"It doesn't make sense for us to all stay together, though," said Emiko. "Perhaps break up into smaller groups."

"And decide on assignments, so we don't duplicate our efforts," added Forrest.

Moonbeam smiled and nodded. I could see she was pleased that Forrest was getting involved.

"So what places are best for gathering local gossip?" asked Glo. "Maybe a salon? Who needs a haircut?"

"Oh, pick me!" said Sebastian, raising his hand. "I love salons and I love gossip!" He ran his raised hand over his already perfectly coiffed hair. "And I could definitely use a haircut."

"Hardly," said Frank, covering his words with a cough.

I was still surprised that local people seemed not to notice that one member of our group was a talking cat. I guess it was that fictional community in a book thing. It was odd because most everything here seemed perfectly normal otherwise.

"How about a diner?" asked Zell. "Lots of locals in a place like that."

"But we're already eating," said Vee.

"I could go for pie and coffee," said Zell. "Maybe stop at that nice Birdies Bakery, too?"

"I'll go with you!" volunteered Emiko. "I love pie and pastries."

The two of them happily fist-bumped.

"We need some groceries," said Moonbeam. "I spotted a community market that looked full of local produce."

"That's good," I agreed.

Moonbeam looked at her son with hope in her eyes. "Do you want to go with me, Forrest?"

"Yeah, sure," he said, stuffing another chip and salsa into his mouth.

Moonbeam glowed with happiness.

The server returned with a helper, and they passed out all our food. Everyone happily dug into their meals.

"What are the rest of you going to do?" asked Emiko.

"I'd like to find the town hall or a visitors' bureau," I said. "I want to know about this Changing Season Festival that's advertised on flyers all over the place. It seems like an opportunity to get a handle on the town."

"Oh, yeah," said Glo. "Good idea, Paige. I'll go with you for that."

"I think I'll just wander around the town," said Vee. "We passed by a big park. That might be a good spot to scope out the people."

"I'll hang out with Vee," said Frank. "I like parks and I like wandering around."

"No chasing birds," warned Zell.

"As if I would do such a thing," huffed Frank.

We finished up lunch, then agreed to meet at the van at five o'clock sharp to head back to the inn to share information in a book club meeting.

~ ~ ~

The hostess at the restaurant had given me directions to the town hall. Glo and I strolled the block, staring at the surroundings in awe. As Zell had said, this author took descriptions seriously and apparently had an addiction to adjectives. The shops weren't just nice, they were brimming with charm. The flower baskets throughout town were abundant and vibrant. The shop owners and townspeople were cheerful and friendly.

"Everything is a little bit ... more than it should be. You know what I mean?" asked Glo.

"I was just thinking the same thing. It's like Disneyland came in and enhanced a Hallmark town."

We both laughed until I abruptly stopped.

"Will that mean that the murder is also over the top?"

Glo's eyes bugged out. "Yeah. Like a naked dead man crammed into a wire animal trap?"

"We should keep an open mind. The rules of normal life may not apply here. Hey – here's the town hall."

We entered the building and found a small one-room office with two clerks busy at work.

"Hi! Can I help you?" asked one of the clerks. The other one smiled and waved at us from the back of the room.

I noticed a few more posters on the walls announcing the Changing Season Festival.

"We're new in town and are wondering about the festival."

"Oh! You're new! You must be part of the group of folks living up at the inn?"

"Yep, that's us." Glo pointed at the two of us and smiled. "Our friends are wandering around getting to know the town."

"We have a festival for each changing season. There's food and contests. Rides for the kids – and fun-loving adults, too! Everybody goes. It takes place in the acreage behind the main park downtown. Plenty of room to run! We'd love to '*see you*' there – if you know what I mean!" She had used finger quotes around the words *see you.*

"We'll be there!" Glo said.

We left the building and I turned toward Glo. "What was with her accent on the words '*see you'?"*

She chuckled and her eyebrows twitched. "Maybe it's a nudist colony?"

"Stop it!" I covered my face and blushed, then we both laughed.

21

We were finding our seats in the book club library, which took longer than one might think. The group had meandered down the stairs chit-chatting like old friends, but like old friends, there were a few minor squabbles over who would sit where. Finally, we were all settled.

"Aren't you supposed to bang the gavel to call the meeting to order?" asked Frank.

"You don't 'bang' it," said Emiko. "It's more like a tap. My toastmaster group leader said you shouldn't frighten your audience into silence and try to break the lectern, but give a firm tap to signal the start of the meeting."

"I don't have a lectern or a gavel," I pointed out.

"You can use an alternative," Emiko said. "Usually something appropriate to the group."

"How about a book?" said Forrest. "Since it's a book club."

"That could be construed as disrespectful," said Glo. "How about a pen?"

"Anybody have a pen?" said Moonbeam, looking around the room.

Zell let out a big huff. "We've never done any of that before. The group leader just starts talking. Paige, you can just start talking, no big announcement required."

"Ack. You're no fun," said Frank. "I had them all going there."

I rapped my knuckle twice on the coffee table.

"Who's there?" said Frank.

I rolled my eyes. "I'd like to call this meeting to order!"

Everyone stopped talking and snapped their heads up to look at me. I smiled at my success.

"The books about our mystery were sitting on the coffee table today when I came down here." I brought out the stack of eight books tied together with twine.

"That's fantastic!" hooted Sebastian. "Now we can find out what happens and get out of here!"

My unhappy expression gave me away and I shook my head. Sebastian deflated.

"Well ... not exactly. I looked through a book, and it's being written as we go."

"What do you mean?"

I untied the twine and held up the top copy. I flipped through the second half of the book, holding it up so everyone could see the blank white pages. I flipped to the last page of written material.

"The last page that has type on it is about what is happening right now. We're in the library having a book club meeting. Look. In the story, I just flipped open the book and showed you the blank pages."

Vee whistled. "That is the weirdest thing I've heard yet."

"Weirder than a dead guy in a cage?" said Forrest.

"Touché. The second weirdest thing," said Vee.

"So, what's the point of the eight books, then?" asked Emiko.

"Remember what we said before?" said Zell. "They're like keepsakes. Like ... umm ... your vacation journal!"

"Plus, sometimes we go back and review chapters or scenes when we're solving the mystery," said Frank.

"Why didn't you guys tell us any of this before?" asked Sebastian.

Frank and Zell both shrugged. "You didn't ask," said Zell.

"It would be great if everyone shared anything new that they learned today," I said. "Why don't we start with Sebastian. Your hair looks great, by the way."

"Thanks, Paige. The salon was a hotbed of gossip! Everyone was talking about Randall Ward's murder. Just like the neighbors said, nobody liked him. He was a recluse and a slob. The river pollution is a super big deal for these people, being out in the country, you know. Nobody seemed the least bit bothered by his death, though. I'm beginning to think his nickname is Skunk, or maybe that's just what they called him behind his back, since more than one person referred to him that way."

"That's not a stretch; sounds like he earned the name. Any possible leads for suspects?" asked Glo.

"I think we're on the right track to take a closer look at everyone who lives along the river," said Sebastian. "They'd be most affected by this, right?"

Emiko shook her head. "I can't imagine anyone we met today doing *that* to Randall Ward, no matter how much they hated him."

I turned to the white board. "Why don't we list the people we met? They could be suspects – or they could lead us to suspects. Let's not get hung up on guilt or innocence now. Let's not get emotional. It's just a list of people."

"Makes sense," said Zell.

"You're supposed to put a box with the victim's name in the middle. Put the suspects around him," said Frank. "Draw him in a cage." He snickered.

I drew a box in the middle and wrote *Randall Ward, victim.* Then I made a box in the top corner.

"Who'd we meet first?"

"Officer Carter Sandoval," said Emiko in a small voice.

Moonbeam opened her mouth to speak and I shook my head at her. I knew she was about to spout something about Emiko liking Carter. That was a dead end, so best left alone. I wrote his name on the board without comment and drew another box.

We thought about everyone we'd met and soon had all the names on the board:

Officer Carter Sandoval
Duchess (Carter's daughter)
Selena and Brandy
Outlaw and Cheyenne Swiftwater (Brandy's parents)
Jeremiah and Daisy Remlinger

"It's a starting point," Glo pointed out.

"Let's get back to our recon today," I suggested.

"Oooo! Recon! Good word," said Frank.

"Did anyone else learn something of value today?" I scanned the faces of the club members.

"Zell and I went to the diner," said Emiko.

"We learned they have great apple pie!" said Zell.

Emiko cleared her throat and tried to sound serious. "We also heard people talking about the murder. Ditto that nobody liked the victim. There was no sadness or fond memories. Just stories about what a weirdo he was."

"Yeah. Nobody said a good word about him," said Zell.

"We also stopped by Birdie's Bakery again," said Emiko. "The owner told us a little more about Randall Ward. He was divorced like twenty years ago. Sounds like he had a couple of kids who are adults now. He's estranged from them, it appears, since nobody ever saw a visitor there. She said maybe it's a case of them wanting to get their hands on the property. Waterfront property is pricey, and if his place were cleaned up it would be a beautiful spot. And inheritance is a common murder motive."

"Oh, nice work Emiko!" said Sebastian, clapping his hands.

"And Zell," grumbled Zell.

"And you too, Zell," I quickly amended. "Emiko, can you follow up and find out who his kids are and where they live, that kind of thing?"

"Easy-peasy," she said.

Glo spoke up next and shared what we'd learned about the festival. "The lady at the town hall told us that everybody goes. It's a big local event. We could scope out tons of people. It's tomorrow evening. I think we should definitely go."

"A festival! How fun," said Moonbeam. "I love fairs and festivals. I wonder if they'll have—"

"Vee and Frank," I jumped in before we got sidetracked on the festival. "Did the two of you spot anything interesting?"

"At least five species of birds," said Frank. "An abundance of squirrels, a couple of chipmunks, and a very nice hot dog vendor."

"I mean, did you spot anything pertinent to the murder mystery? Vee?"

"Oh, sure, just skip right over the cat and go directly to the human being. That's discriminatory," complained Frank.

"It's efficient. Vee, anything to report?"

"The hot dog vendor was actually quite helpful —"

"See," interrupted Frank. "Told ya."

"He also talked about Randall Ward being

disliked," said Vee. "You know small towns, everyone knows everyone. But no one really knew him. I guess you could call him an outcast."

"Thanks for sharing. What about you, Moonbeam?"

"I met the nicest couple at the market! Leaf and Serenity. They told me that the local farmers have a market downtown every weekend and the whole street gets closed down to traffic. We'll have to check that out."

"That's it?" I asked.

Moonbeam squirmed.

"Mom, you have to tell them." Forrest sounded annoyed.

"Tell them what, Forrest?" She said his name as if scolding him.

"Fine. I'll tell them. Those people my mom met —"

"Forrest! You don't know anything. They were very nice!" Moonbeam eyes shined with tears.

"You think they were just like you with their hippie clothes and their cloth grocery bags and their love of the farmer's market. They were nothing like you!" Forrest turned to us.

"When my mom was talking to them at the register, I saw the guy pull out his wallet for his credit card. I saw on his driver's license that his real name isn't Leaf, it's Yuma Tanaka. When we got back home, I Googled him. He and his wife Akemi have been arrested a bunch of times for picketing against local businesses. He chained himself to the front door of the grocery store until they promised to stop using plastic bags. They broke the windows in a shop that sold leather goods. They even started a fire in front of a gun shop and wrote on the building in paint."

"Forrest! You didn't tell me you spied on them!"

Moonbeam looked angry.

"It's not spying, Moonbeam," interjected Glo. "He was appropriately researching for our story."

"Behind my back!" She raised her voice.

"Hey!" said Sebastian, pointing at Moonbeam. "You can't be keeping secrets like this! We need everything we can get to finish this case and go home!"

"You're getting in the way of our escape," Vee said with a scowl.

Moonbeam stood up and put her hands on her hips. "Are you accusing me of—"

There was a yowl of distress, and then a thud.

Frank lay on the floor. His eyes were closed, his body as limp as a ragdoll.

22

"Oh my God! Frank!" Glo moved so fast she nearly flew.

"What happened! Oh, no! Is he dead?" Moonbeam stared at the limp cat and started to cry.

Glo and Sebastian hovered over Frank trying to find a pulse. "Where's his pulse? Does anyone know how to do CPR on a cat?"

"Call 9-1-1!" shouted Emiko.

"Got it!" yelled Forrest. He dialed and spoke quickly to the operator. "They said call an animal hospital!"

I grabbed my phone and with shaking hands typed *animal hospital near me*. I saw the closest one and hit dial. It was an after-hours recording with an emergency number.

"I need a pen!" I shouted. Someone handed me a pen, I didn't even know who. I re-dialed and wrote the emergency number on my arm, then made the call to the Ants to Zebras Animal Hospital emergency line. I described the problem and realized I had no idea what our address was. I gave our location as two doors down from Randall Ward's house.

"Are you the people at the new inn?" asked the woman on the line.

"Yes! That's us!"

"Is your cat breathing? Is there a pulse? Is it fast or slow?"

"Yes, he's breathing. How do we take his pulse?"

The woman was calm and steady. "Roll your cat over on the side. Feel between the shoulder blade and chest."

I repeated this to Sebastian, who followed the directions.

"Yes! There's a pulse!" he called out. "It seems normal, I think."

I relayed the information to the woman from the animal hospital.

"She said they can send someone in a half hour," I called out, "or we can drive to them. They're downtown. Not far from the Mexican restaurant."

"We are not waiting!" said Glo, jumping up off the floor. "I'll pull the van out by the front door. Put Frank in a box or on something, cover him with a blanket, and meet me out front." Glo ran up the stairs.

Everyone scurried about. Sebastian and I continued to monitor Frank. Emiko ran upstairs and brought back a cardboard box. Forrest followed her and returned with a couple of blankets. We lined the box with a blanket and carefully moved Frank, then covered him with the smaller blanket. Sebastian carried the box upstairs and we quickly got into the van. Glo was driving out before the door was fully closed.

Sebastian and Emiko sat on either side of the box. Emiko laid her hand on Frank's back, her other hand underneath him on his chest. The rest of us continued to lean over the seats to check on the cat.

We were silent on the drive except for Moonbeam's quiet crying, Forrest's calming words whispered to his mother, and Emiko's reassuring voice every few minutes reporting that Frank's heartbeat still felt good.

We arrived at the animal hospital and Glo pulled the van right up onto the grass in front of the door. We filed into the office and a woman with a stethoscope around her neck met us in the lobby and directed us to an examination room. We barely fit elbow to elbow in the small space.

A second woman with a lab coat came into the room. Moonbeam's sniffling and everyone else's vibrating concern were quite distracting, not to mention being scrunched into the exam room. I wasn't surprised when she very politely said, "Can I ask all of you to go sit in the waiting room?"

We reluctantly left Frank in their – hopefully – capable hands.

There were plenty of chairs in the waiting room, but most of us were pacing. Everyone kept glancing at the closed door where Frank was being cared for. There was no one at the reception desk, so we were left alone to worry.

"Can cats have heart attacks?" asked Emiko.

"I don't know!" Glo responded in a panicked voice. Vee went to stand by Glo and put an arm around her shoulders.

"I'll look it up," said Forrest. He tapped on his phone then stared at his screen. He jammed his phone in his pocket without answering the question. He didn't say a word, so we knew what that meant.

That ratcheted up Moonbeam's sniffling to a full-out cry. She fell back onto a chair and Forrest sat beside her, rubbing her back and making shushing sounds.

Zell was sitting in a chair, rocking herself back and forth and wringing her hands. I sat beside her and took her shaking hands in mine.

"I'm sure he'll be okay," I said, even though I had no idea if that was true. "He's in good hands." I didn't know if that was true, either. This whole town was new to me, and I didn't know what would happen next in our story, or if this was even a scripted part of it. I didn't know if we drove the story, or the story drove us.

I looked around the room and spied thank you notes posted on a large bulletin board. There were photos of cats, dogs, rabbits, horses, and parrots. The photos even included wild animals. I saw deer, raccoons, and an eagle. This small-town office apparently took care of all creatures – big and small, domestic and wild.

It seemed like we were waiting for a horribly long time. I looked at the clock and was surprised to see it was only a half hour. The door opened and the veterinarian came out into the waiting room.

"Frank is going to be just fine," she said with a smile.

"Did he have a heart attack?" asked Forrest.

"No, he didn't have a heart attack. I saw no signs of any serious health problem. It could have been a panic attack, though."

"A panic attack?" shrieked Zell. "What does Frank have to be anxious about? He's the one who makes us anxious!"

"Just like with humans, a cat can respond to high levels of stress with a mild seizure that can cause their heart rate to race, and it can cause trembling and vomiting."

"Can it make them pass out?" asked Zell.

"I suppose it could cause a temporary loss of consciousness," the vet replied. "This kind of reaction could be brought on by a response to a stressful situation."

We all looked at each other, guilt coloring our expressions as we recalled our arguments in the library just before Frank passed out.

"Is Frank awake?" I asked. "Can we go in and see him?"

"Yes, you may, but please keep it calm and quiet.

I'd like him to remain stabilized for a bit before I'm comfortable sending him home."

We all squeezed into the small examination room. Frank was lying on the exam table looking weak and sleepy.

"Oh, Frankie!" said Zell. She laid her hand on him and stoked his soft fur.

Frank gave a little moan and looked at us through his mostly closed eyes.

"Hey guys," Glo said. "It's our fault that this happened."

"It's all our fault!" wailed Zell. "The poor little guy couldn't take it. We need to keep our control. No more of this fighting nonsense. We're a team!"

"You're right," said Moonbeam. "I feel terrible for getting so upset. Forrest, honey, I'm sorry I got mad at you."

"That's okay, Mom," said Forrest. "It's your good heart. You always believe the best of people."

"We need to work together on this mystery," I said. "We have a lot of great people in this group, and I know if we put our heads together, we can figure this out."

"I agree," said Vee. "We all have talents we can use to solve the mystery and get us back home." She was standing next to Emiko who voiced her agreement, as well. The two of them slung their arms around each other.

Sebastian went over to stand next to Moonbeam. "I'm so sorry I yelled at you, Moonbeam. I've been incredibly stressed over this whole thing. I didn't mean to take it out on you."

"I know, honey," said Moonbeam squeezing his hand. "We're all feeling the stress right now."

"There you go!" said Frank, sitting up on the table. "I knew you guys would work this out!" He pumped one furry fist in the air.

"Frank?" Zell's brows knit together, and her lips pursed. "Were you *faking?*"

"You heard the doctor," said Frank in an oddly strong voice. "It could have been an anxiety attack. Brought on by all the bickering. And you all rushed me here and brought me back from the brink!"

"What brink?" said Vee.

"The brink!" said Frank. "I was on the edge. I was —"

"There is nothing wrong with you!" said Zell. "Admit it!"

Frank let out a huge sigh. "Okay, fine. There's nothing wrong with me. Guilty as charged. You must admit, though, my acting skills are pretty dang good, right?"

Everyone was glaring at the cat.

"And hey, you've learned that the best plan is to all work together to solve the mystery. I think I deserve a standing ovation."

There was a moment of complete silence, then Moonbeam started to laugh. Then she began to slowly clap her hands.

Vee shook her head and joined in the slow applause. In a manner of minutes, we were all applauding Frank's act. Then we started laughing. It appeared that the cat had manipulated all of us into working together as a stronger, more focused team.

"Well played, Frank." I said between chuckles. "Well played."

23

"G'morning, Glo. Are you the only one up?" I yawned and stretched as I entered the kitchen where Glo was making coffee.

"Yeah. I think all the trauma over Frank's fake heart attack knocked them out." She chuckled.

I laughed, too. "That little stinker. I can't believe he had us all in a tizzy."

"We'll have to keep an eye on him." Glo motioned out the window at the sunny morning. "It's a beautiful morning. Want to take a walk?"

I glanced outside and was once again jarred by the view. It still hadn't sunk in. It seemed so weird to look out the inn window and not see the same yard that existed my whole life at GeeGee's house.

"When I look outside it's like my daily morning reminder that we aren't in Kansas anymore. Well, Colorado."

"I don't know. It's pretty cool, right?" said Glo. "I'm starting to adapt to the whole book idea."

"You would!" I shook my head at my adventurous aunt. She was always up for something new, and that definitely fit our current predicament.

"Do you want tea or coffee before our walk?" she asked. "I just started making a pot."

"No, thanks. Then I'll just have to pee. I'll have something when we get back."'

"Good point. Let me grab a sweater and we can go."

We strolled down the lovely country lane, spying the river in the background behind the homes. I was looking through to the gardens at Jeremiah and Daisy's home when I spotted two people walking along the fence.

"Hey, look." I pointed as the two people shoved through a break in the fence.

We stopped walking and watched.

"Isn't that Jeremiah and Daisy?" asked Glo.

"Yeah, it is! Why are they cutting through the fence onto Randall Ward's property? Why wouldn't they go through the front if they need to be over there? Honestly, though, it seems odd that they'd even be there, right? Especially given the owner is ... umm ... gone."

"You mean dead. And it's so early. No one else is around. Should we go investigate?"

"Glo! It's not our business."

"Yeah, it is. We're supposed to solve the mystery, right? And apparently, we are where we should be, which means it was meant for us to see them. Stands to reason we'd go see what's up."

"That's some weird reasoning. I'm shocked that it makes sense. Okay, let's do it."

We walked through the Remlinger's yard up to the area of fence that they'd climbed through.

"After you," I said.

"Big baby!" accused Glo as she confidently charged through the break in the fence.

We spotted the couple. They were looking through the vegetation near the shed where we'd discovered the body.

"Hello!" called Glo.

"What are you doing?" I whispered to her.

"Follow my lead," she said.

"Glo? Paige?" said Daisy. "Why are you back here?"

"We're trying to find our cat, Frank. He got out this morning and I thought he might have gone through the yards."

"Really?" said Jeremiah. "What a coincidence. We're trying to find our cat, too."

I glanced at Glo and mouthed, *What?!*

"Must be the day of loose cats!" laughed Glo. "Have you seen ours?"

"Nope," said Jeremiah. "We'll let you know if we spot him."

"What does your cat look like?" I asked, then added, "so we know what to look for."

"He's a gray tabby," said Daisy.

"What's his name?" I asked.

She laughed. "We just call him Cat. We'll keep an eye out for Frank for you."

"Okay, thanks," Glo said.

The two of us walked back out to the street.

"Not suspicious at all," I said.

"Right. A gray tabby named Cat. How original." Glo looked proud. "See, I told you we were meant to be there. It's like the author was saying, 'Look! Suspects!'"

"Why do you think they were really over there?" I asked.

"Maybe they left a clue and wanted it gone before the police found it. They dropped a necklace or a shoe or something?"

"A shoe?"

She put her hands on her hips. "Yeah. A shoe."

I held my gut and bent over with laughter. "I think you've been reading too many mysteries lately."

She snorted. "You should be glad that I have. I have some very good mystery-solving skills."

"Let's go back and see if everyone is awake. We can tell them about the missing shoe." I snickered.

~ ~ ~

"Yeah. Of course. A shoe," said Zell, confirming Glo's hypothesis. "A common item left behind. Perhaps stuck in the mud, or one that fell off when the perp ran away from the scene of the homicide."

"The perp! The scene of the homicide!" parroted Sebastian. "We sound like real detectives."

"Are you starting to have *fun*?" asked Moonbeam with a smirk.

Sebastian gasped. "Oh, blimey! I guess I am!"

"Blimey?" said Frank, strolling into the kitchen where the rest of us had gathered. "Since when are you an old English bloke?"

"Trying it out. You like it?"

"Nah. Doesn't suit you. It's better than *goodness, gracious, deary me!* But if you don't want to sound like a lady from the 1800s you can say *oh, wow, that's poggers.*"

"Poggers?" asked Sebastian.

"Means amazing, cool, excellent," said Frank.

"Who says poggers?" asked Zell.

"People in the know," said Frank.

Zell scrunched up her face. "Sounds fishy to me."

"Can we get back to talking about the case?" I asked.

"Sounds poggers to me," said Moonbeam. Frank and Sebastian nodded in approval.

Zell put up her hand. "Before we do, there's something important we must address."

That caught everyone's attention.

"What are we going to make for breakfast?"

"Right! Breakfast," agreed Emiko.

"I vote for pancakes," said Forrest, looking up from his phone for just a moment.

"Do we have any bacon?" asked Vee, opening the refrigerator and rooting around.

"Who wants a smoothie?" Moonbeam asked, already removing the lid to her juicer.

I groaned. Then I plunked down on a chair and slowly raised my hand, "Me."

~ ~ ~

At the rate we were going it would take a month to solve the mystery and get through this book. Every meal was a major to-do, and every conversation took a dozen detours. Once everyone was about done eating breakfast, I banged my fork on the table twice.

"Who's there?" said Zell, Frank, Moonbeam, and Sebastian in unison. Then Sebastian had to get up out of his seat and run about and fist-bump the peanut gallery.

I thumped the fork only once, then said, "This book club meeting is called to order."

I filled the group in on the story about Daisy and Jeremiah that morning. When I got to the part that we told them Frank was lost, and that's why we were in their yard, Frank hissed and fluffed out his tail.

"I am deeply offended. This cat does not get lost."

"Come on, Frank," said Glo. "Take one for the team."

He sat back down and began to groom his paw. "Fine. Whatever."

"I think we need to step up our game," I said. "We have a list of possible suspects, but we may be missing others. I suggest we head back into town and continue our investigation."

"And what about those plastic eggs?" asked Forrest. "Nobody's talking about those. But that was pretty weird."

"Forrest has a good point," said Glo. "Is there any significance to those eggs? Keep on the lookout for those when we're in town. It's not Easter, so if we find any it could be a valuable tip."

"And then tomorrow is the festival!" said Moonbeam with excitement in her voice.

"Uh, Moonbeam. With all due respect, we're not here to have fun, you know," said Emiko. "We need to attend the festival as part of our investigation."

"Why can't we do both?" said Moonbeam. "I suggest we take a vote." She raised her hand.

"I vote for fun!" said Sebastian, raising his hand, too.

"Me, too!" said Zell, with both hands swaying in the air.

"Yeah," said Forrest, one hand up, which earned him a smile from his mother.

"Okay, okay, fine!" I jumped in. "We'll have fun ... and we'll investigate."

There was a cheer and some applause. This group was going to be the death of me.

I knocked the fork on the table – just once. "Meeting adjourned. Let's head back to town and see what we can learn."

"Can we go to lunch?" asked Zell.

"Zell, we just ate breakfast," said Vee.

"Thinking ahead, my dear girl."

"How about a stop at Birdie's Bakery?" I suggested.

There was more cheering.

24

"How should we approach our research in town today?" I threw the question out to the group.

There were some ideas and discussion, and then Forrest interrupted us.

"Hey. This is the weirdest thing ever," he said. "I was able to Google a local map by typing in *restaurants near me*. It shows the town name as Clarksville, but outside our neighborhood and the downtown area the map just isn't there. It's white space."

"That's because the author didn't describe anything beyond the town itself," said Zell.

"So why do I have wireless and Google? All my games show up, too." Forrest looked as confused as I felt.

"There must be cell service mentioned in the book. Try looking up MSN or CNN."

Forrest looked up with a puzzled look on his face. "Error message. This page is not available. With that cloud thing and a slash through it."

"Figured," said Zell. "Try *Clarksville News.*"

Forrest laughed. "Yeah. It's here. Like a real small-town page. The cover story is the festival. No national or international news."

"Lots of mystery authors don't like to bring depressing world news into their stories. It interrupts the reader's experience," said Moonbeam. "One of the reasons I enjoy cozy mysteries so much."

"If we do this again, let's make sure it's a cozy mystery," I said.

"Aha!" said Frank. "Did you all hear that? Paige is

already planning to go into another book!"

"I said *if*."

"Yeah," said Frank. "You've already considered doing this again. Caught ya."

I shrugged and returned to Forrest's discovery. "It's great that you found a map," I said. "Let's sketch it out and plan a route around town. Want to break down into groups again?"

"This is about to get realllly boring," said Frank. "I'm going to take a nap. See the lot of you later."

With that, Frank went off to find a sunny spot to snooze in.

"Can we all start at the bakery and then go from there?" Emiko asked.

"Has Zell converted you?" Glo wagged her finger at Zell who lifted her hands and laughed.

Emiko chuckled. "Yeah, I guess so! But you must admit, Birdie's Bakery is awesome."

We drew out maps and planned routes for everyone. We went through the bathroom runs, the sweater-finding, and the *oh forgot my purse* drill. Finally, we were in the van heading to town.

We parked close to the Mexican restaurant since it sat in the middle of town. We nearly had to drag Zell away from it. The only reason we succeeded was that we were going to the bakery first.

Walking into Birdie's Bakery, we were greeted with the fragrance of freshly baked goods and a smiling blue-haired lady who waved at us. A tall man at the counter, wearing the local uniform of jeans and a cowboy hat, took a bag and a cup of coffee from Birdie, then turned around.

"Good afternoon, new neighbors." He touched the brim of his hat with the hand that held the bag.

"Carter! Hi!" said Emiko, showing off dimples that I never knew she had.

"Hi, Emiko." He smiled at her and held up his bag. "Birdie makes the best cinnamon scones. You should try them." His eyes took in the rest of us, then landed back on Emiko. "I'll be outside having my coffee. Y'all join me, if you have time."

"Will do! Be right out," said Moonbeam with a cheery voice.

Carter stepped out the door and I saw him take a seat at a round table under a bright blue umbrella.

"Oh, my," said Birdie, fanning herself. "That Officer Carter is a catch. I suspect no lady's caught him yet because he has that Outlaw Swiftwater working on his property." She shivered and shook her head. "I hear he has a police record a mile long and originally started working there as part of his community service. I suppose it's some kind of rehabilitation program."

She looked up at our shocked expressions. "Oh, dear! I've said too much! For a moment I forgot you've moved in right next door to him." She flapped her hands. "I'm sure it's fine. It's fine! He's been here for years with no problems. You guys are safe; he probably won't strike again! Now what can I get you? As Carter says, the scones are good today. Have a sample." She pulled out a tray of Birdie's Bits and offered the crumb-filled muffin cups to the group.

"But fresh scones don't leave crumbs when you bake them," said Moonbeam.

Birdie laughed. "Okay, you caught me. I crumbled some up for sampling."

I caught Glo's eye, and we had a silent conversation. This was an interesting bit of background which made Outlaw even more of a potential suspect.

As always, it was a bit of a circus getting everyone to make their selections and pay for their purchases. As part of our "being in the book" thing we all found enough money in our wallets to sustain us during this trip. I'd have to deal with making some real money when we got back home.

"Emiko, why don't you sit here next to me?" Moonbeam had been the first one outside and was seated next to Carter. As soon as Emiko walked up, she scooted over and made room for Emiko to sit between her and Carter.

I caught Moonbeam's eye and shook my head, warning her to stop matchmaking. She pretended not to see me.

We enjoyed our treats, everyone sharing pieces of their goodies and exclaiming over each pastry.

"So, Carter, I have a question about the festival," I said. "I noticed that it starts at five p.m. That seems late for a community event. Is that so people can come after work?"

"That might be a reason," he answered, nodding. Then he popped the last bite of scone into his mouth, stood up, and tossed the bag and his cup into the trash. "You folks have a great day."

"Hey, is that Daisy?" Vee pointed across the street.

"It certainly is!" said Moonbeam. "Why's she going into a gun store?"

"I say we find out," said Zell. "Who's with me?"

"I'm not going in there," said Moonbeam, getting up in a huff. She threw her bag away, then sat on a wooden bench that was set up near a lamppost next door to Birdie's.

"I'll go," Vee said. "We probably don't want a big group going in there anyhow. I can check it out."

"I'll go with you," I volunteered.

"Me, too," said Glo.

"I'm with you guys," said Zell.

"The rest of us can get started on our routes," said Emiko. "Come on Moonbeam. Let's go explore."

The group split up and the four of us went into the gun shop. It was a small place so we could see the whole shop from the doorway. Daisy was at the counter talking to a clerk. She was examining a rifle, and we could hear their conversation. We all pretended to be engaged in shopping around the store.

"I'm doing everything I can to increase our level of protection," Daisy said.

"Yeah, I know you are," said the clerk. "Hey, you got any new antlers?"

"Oh! I got me a beautiful eight-point buck," Daisy said with pride.

"'What are you gonna do with all the new ones?" he asked.

"Was thinking I might create some kind of decoration for the front porch railings."

Zell moved closer to me and Glo. She lowered her voice to a whisper. "She was lying to us! She shot those deer! I knew it! If she did and she lied to us about that, what else do you think she's capable of doing?" She glanced over at Daisy who was now discussing the rifle with the clerk. "Liars are always good suspects," she said.

At that moment the clerk called out, "Hello! I'll be with y'all in a moment."

Daisy turned around and spotted us. Zell picked up the closest thing to her, a camouflaged vest. She waved it at Daisy.

"Just shopping for a vest!" Zell called out.

"That would look good on you," said Daisy with a grin.

Zell was fast on her feet; I'd give her that. She tried on the vest, which was about five sizes too large. Then she made a big point about it and announced that we'd best get on to the rest of our shopping. Daisy turned around and said goodbye as we headed out to explore more of the town.

The group reconvened at the van after our explorations. Moonbeam was juggling four large grocery bags from the natural food market.

"I'm making us dinner!" she announced.

"Oh! I'll help," said Sebastian. "I love to cook."

"Me, too," said Vee.

"You love to cook?" he looked shocked. "Really?"

"Yeah, I love to cook," she said. "Never judge a book by its cover." She crossed her tattooed arms and quirked a brow at him.

"Oh, I'm so sorry!" He covered his mouth. "That was phenomenally rude of me. I look forward to preparing dinner with you, Vee."

"Thanks, hon." She smiled at him.

Phew. For the sake of Frank's health, I was glad they worked through that quickly.

~ ~ ~

The kitchen was bustling with way too many people, making tea and coffee, and filling water glasses, but Moonbeam, Sebastian and Vee didn't seem to mind.

They worked together smoothly as they created a feast for our dinner.

Moonbeam took the first dish to the table. “Everybody take a seat! This is baked chicken with fresh rosemary. Don’t worry, it’s made with ‘happy chicken.’”

“What’s ‘happy chicken’?” asked Emiko.

“That’s when they are raised humanely. They come from free-range farms and are fed wholesome food.”

“Before they’re butchered,” said Vee under her breath.

“Humanely!” said Forrest. “They gave up their happy lives so we can have this delicious meal.”

“Forrest!” exclaimed Moonbeam.

“Well, people have to eat, Mom. We can’t live on lettuce alone!”

Sebastian put an end to the conversation by adding two large bowls to the table. “Orange fennel salad and red potato salad.”

Vee added the last tray, announcing, “Roasted broccoli with garlic and parmesan cheese.”

“Everything looks amazing,” said Glo. “Thanks, you guys.”

We passed around the food and everyone showered the cooks with well-deserved praise.

“Does anyone have news from your time in town?” I asked.

“Those tree-huggers were back at the market,” said Forrest.

Moonbeam gave him a look.

“I mean, those environmentally conscious folks were back at the market.”

“Leaf and Serenity,” said Moonbeam.

“Yuma and Akemi Tanaka,” said Forrest, without looking at his mother. “They were set up at a table out front with a petition trying to get people to sign it.”

"Did you talk to them?" I asked.

"We did," said Moonbeam. "I asked them what they knew about the river pollution." She looked at her son with what seemed to be a bit of pride. "Forrest was right! They got very angry and up in arms about it. They said that if the town didn't step up and get it cleaned up right away then they would 'see to it.' That's how he put it, they'd 'see to it.' They said, 'we're people of action, we don't wait around.' But then other people came up and so we left. They did seem like the kind of people who would go to extremes – and break laws."

"Good work," I told them. "We'll add their names to the suspect list. Forrest, can you see what else you can learn about them?"

"For sure." He nodded.

I told the group about seeing Carter at the bakery and Birdie's information about Outlaw actually being an outlaw. Then Glo shared the story of Daisy in the gun shop.

"We're firming up that suspect list!" said Zell, happily devouring her dinner. "Yummy. This is as good as restaurant food," she said.

"If Carter has a convict working for him, is he someone with a good heart who provided a second chance to a criminal, or did they work together to kill Randall Ward?" asked Sebastian. "And is Daisy a sweet, innocent deer killer, or a man killer?"

"Those are the right questions," I said. "Now we need to find the answers."

25

Our morning breakfast hubbub was interrupted by the doorbell gong.

"Got it," said Moonbeam, jumping up off her chair.

We heard the front door open and a deep voice.

"Come on in, Carter," said Moonbeam. "Want to join us for some breakfast? Coffee?"

"Coffee would be great," he said. He stepped into the kitchen. "Good morning, folks!" He took off his cowboy hat and graced us with a kind smile.

Moonbeam asked, "Cream or sugar?"

"Sugar, three cubes," he answered. "Sorry to disturb your morning. I have some news about Randall Ward's death and I'm out chatting with all the neighbors. Do you have a few minutes?"

"Certainly," I said. I turned to the cluster in the kitchen. "Can everyone have a seat at the table, please." I looked at Carter. "With this group it's easier to hold their attention that way."

Carter smiled, then walked over to pet Frank who was sitting on the counter. "How ya doing, Frank?"

"Not bad. Yourself?" asked Frank.

"Fine."

"How's that sick foal getting along?"

"Improving," said Carter. "The vet came by this morning and said he looks good. Thanks again for letting me know that you thought he looked sick."

"No problem."

Our heads were bouncing back and forth from one to the other. What the heck? Apparently when we weren't looking, Frank was out making more friends in the neighborhood.

Frank and Carter continued to talk about the sick horse while the group did their usual pre-activity tasks: bathroom runs, sweater-getting, refilling coffee and teacups. At long last, everyone was seated.

Carter grabbed a seat at the head of the table. "We received the coroner's report on Randall Ward. He was killed with a healthy dose of anticoagulant. That's a pesticide used to get rid of rats, mice, and other rodents. He was put into the cage either unconscious or dead. A live man would not have been able to fit inside the trap, unless he was a contortionist, which Ward was not."

"That's horrible!" said Moonbeam with a grimace.

"Is it though?" said Zell. "I mean, everybody and his mother hated the guy. And since he was polluting the river, it put an end to that drama. Seems like no great loss to the community."

"Zell! He was still a human being," said Moonbeam.

"Not a good one, though," she huffed.

Carter interrupted. "We've had no other instances like this, so it's unlikely you're in danger. However, there is a murderer in our community, and it did happen on our street. We're asking all residents to report anything they see or hear that is suspicious or concerning."

"Would a woman with an unhealthy passion for her rifle be concerning?" asked Sebastian.

"What do you mean?" Carter asked.

"Daisy Remlinger. We've seen her shooting her pistol and buying a rifle. And she's very upset about the polluted river and how it's affecting her crops."

"The victim didn't die by gunshot," said Carter.

"And Daisy's been having target practice in her yard for years. She's across from a river and a forested hill, so there's no danger to the neighbors. In addition, everyone in the community was unhappy about the river pollution; she's not alone in that."

"What about Outlaw Swiftwater?" asked Moonbeam.

We all gasped. I could see that none of us could believe she even asked a question about Carter's employee.

"What about him?" Carter asked.

"We hear he's a criminal. With a long record," Moonbeam persisted.

We waited for Carter's answer.

"None of Outlaw's criminal charges align with this situation."

Then Carter simply stopped talking and looked Moonbeam in the eye. It was like he was waiting for her next question and prepared to shut her down.

"Are there any questions about *this case*?" He emphasized the words to let us know that he was done talking about his employee.

Forrest spoke up. "There were some sketchy people at the market who are pretty worked up over the river pollution."

"What do you mean?" asked Carter.

"This guy Yuma Tanaka and his wife Akemi have a habit of picketing local businesses. He chained himself to a grocery store one time. They broke the windows in a shop and started a fire in front of another place. A gun store. And they wrote on the building in paint. They were arrested a bunch of times. And yeah, they are crazy angry over the river and said if the city doesn't clean it up then they'd do something about it. Like I said, they were mad."

"Thanks, Forrest." He took out his phone and

made a note. "Anything else?"

Everyone shook their heads.

"Thanks for your time. If you see anything, let me know."

"I'll see you out," offered Emiko. She stood up and walked him to the door. We heard their low voices out on the porch.

After a few minutes, Emiko stuck her head back inside the door. "I'm going to take a walk with Carter!" she called out.

The door shut, and we all looked at Moonbeam.

"That was gutsy," said Glo. "Bringing up Outlaw like that. I'm impressed."

Sebastian applauded.

Moonbeam took a bow. "Thank you."

~ ~ ~

An hour later Emiko returned to the house. Everyone had scattered to rest up and prepare for the festival. I heard her out on the porch and stepped outside to see her sitting alone on the porch swing. I sat down beside her.

"I can see that you really like Carter."

"I do," she said. "He's amazing. I've never felt like this before. I get butterflies every time I look at him. It's crazy. I mean, I usually date men who are like me – serious, accounting types. We go to movies. We go out to dinner. It's very bland and normal. But Carter is so different! He's exciting and strong, and so good looking." She blushed and looked down at her tightly clasped hands.

"Emiko, you should not let your heart get swept away by him."

"It's too late for that." She smiled, but the expression didn't reach her eyes.

"You know this is temporary. Right? He's a character in a book. We are in a book. When the mystery is solved, we'll go home."

"You mean to tell me you've never fallen in love with a character in a book?" She glanced at me.

"Well, sure. Everybody does. But that's different. It's just a ... umm ... paper infatuation. He's like a real person."

"You just said he was only a character. Now you say he's real."

"I mean he's *like* a real person. But he's not."

"I held his hand. He felt real." She frowned.

"Oh, sweetie." I put my arm around her. "Do you really want to do this to yourself?"

"I'll take what I can get. I'll live in the moment. And then I'll have the mystery book, right? It will all be in the book, like a forever treasured memory I can open and re-read any time I want."

I sat next to Emiko for a while, letting the seat sway gently, allowing her to embrace her memories.

26

"Look! They have a Ferris wheel!" squealed Moonbeam, as if she were a little girl, not a grown woman in a tie-dyed T-shirt and frayed jeans.

Sebastian opened his window and leaned his head out. We could hear the sounds of the festival as we inched forward to a parking spot.

He inhaled deeply. "I can smell the grilled onions from here. I love fair food."

"Me, too," said Forrest. "I hope they have those big turkey legs."

"Only if it's from a happy turkey," said Moonbeam.

"Mom, we're out in the country. I bet all the turkeys are happy."

"Until they're not," said Vee, rolling her eyes.

"Everybody out!" Zell announced. "Let's get this party started."

Of course it was not an easy thing to get this party started. There was a gathering of backpacks, donning sweatshirts, someone stooping to re-tie their shoes, and someone else who was, in fact, changing their shoes. I leaned against the front of the van next to Forrest, who was scrolling on his phone.

"Like herding cats," I mumbled.

"Uh, huh." He didn't even look up.

I took a moment to reflect on the fact that I'd just met these people, yet it felt like I'd known them a lifetime. They were a curious bunch, but every one loveable in their own way. I was grateful to GeeGee for leaving us the house and the library, and for leading us to create the book club. I'm sure she knew exactly what she was doing. I had a feeling – not that I'd tell anyone this out loud – that this group would have many more mystery book adventures together.

"Everybody ready?" asked Glo. "Shall I lock the van?"

There was a chorus of answers, none the same, but it sounded like they were all ready to go.

Frank popped his head out of the backpack that Sebastian was wearing. "Onward fine steed!"

Sebastian reached back and attempted to bop Frank in the head, but Frank kept dodging his hand.

"If you want to keep riding back there, you best be nice to me," said Sebastian.

"I did say *fine* steed, did I not?"

We left the parking area and headed toward the event. Probably a hundred cars were parked, and people were making their way to a front gate. We joined the line to get tickets.

Glo whistled. "This is way more than a small-town festival. It looks like a county fair!"

Zell clapped her hands. "This is fantastic. I love books like this one!"

I shook my head at her reminder that we were in a book. It still seemed impossible. Yet here we were.

"Just like we did in town, I think we should break up into groups so we can cover more ground."

"I want to be with Zell!" said Moonbeam, walking over to put her arm around the little lady.

"Uh uh," I said. "You two will be so distracted by the event you'll be useless as investigators. We're supposed to try to learn about the people; that's why we're here."

Zell put her hands on her hips. "Who among us

is the only human experienced in book travel? And who is the elder of the group? Don't get so big for your britches, young lady. I shall indeed be doing my investigative work with my friend Moonbeam."

"Okay, fine," I said, "but someone else should go with you two."

"I will," said Vee.

"Fine," I reluctantly agreed. I noticed that Vee had a sparkle in her eye, too. So much for the serious biker girl I first met.

"Forrest, you can come with us," said Sebastian, Frank nodding agreement over his shoulder.

"Then Glo and Emiko can work with me," I said.

"Oh, serious Paige! This isn't all about work today. Let down your hair and have yourself a bit of fun today," said Sebastian.

"I thought you were all about getting out of the book?" I asked him, wondering for a moment if I had a bit more of my mother in me than I thought.

He huffed and tutted at me but didn't say anything. I think his own change of attitude caught him off guard.

"Sebby is right," said Zell.

"Who the heck is Sebby?" asked Sebastian.

"You don't like it?"

"No, ma'am."

"Sorry. Sebastian is right," said Zell. "We should have some fun today. It's not like we have to actually solve the mystery."

"Wait! Hold on." We were all walking and I stopped and turned to Zell. "I thought the whole thing was that we have to solve the mystery to get out of the book!"

"Kind of. The mystery must be solved for us to get out. I'm not really sure if our group does the solving. We become part of the characters, and sometimes our parts are bigger than others."

"But you said we have to solve the mystery!" Vee said. "I distinctly remember you saying that."

"Yeah ... 'we' ... as in 'we' the characters in the book. We always go where we go and do what we do and pretty soon – bam! – the mystery is solved, and we go home."

"And if we move things along more quickly, do we get home sooner?"

"Good question!" said Zell, and she turned around and began walking toward the festival.

"You mean you don't know?" I yelled.

"I mean I don't know!" she called back over her shoulder.

We passed through the ticket turnstile and looked around at the bustling festival.

"How about we meet back here at the front gate at eight o'clock?" I suggested. "We can touch base and make a plan for the rest of the night."

"Sounds good," said Glo. "I'm sending a group message now to test the signal."

Everyone's phones beeped. Zell had to find her phone at the bottom of her large canvas bag. Some people set alarms. Moonbeam said she never carried her phone. Two people already asked where the bathrooms were.

"Enough already!" said Frank. "Can we go now, boss lady?"

Glo, Emiko and I wandered the grounds. This was, indeed, very much like a county fair. There were plenty of food booths with all the standard fair food that would surely distract half of the people in our group. A cluster of tents displayed local contest winners' photography, flowers, and baked goods, proudly emphasized by blue ribbons. There was a selection of kids' rides already filled with screeching children. All the usual game booths were featured: balloon pop, basketball nets, ring toss.

"Look!" said Glo. "They have one of those rifle-shooting games. And guess who's playing it?"

I turned to see Daisy taking aim at the target. "Geeze, it's like she's obsessed," Emiko said. "Does that make her a murder suspect?" she whispered.

"It was poison, not a shooting," said Glo. "So, it makes her scary, but not a suspect."

"That doesn't make her a suspect, but her anger over the river does," said Emiko. "And she certainly had the opportunity – living right next door to the victim. And her sneaking in to find her gray tabby cat named Cat. I still don't trust her."

"Birdie has a fair booth!" said Emiko, pointing at a colorful booth advertising scones and cupcakes.

We wandered over to the booth to see Birdie, her children, and a very tall man dressed in standard country-man apparel: jeans, a plaid shirt, and a white cowboy hat.

"Hi, Birdie!" I called out.

Her face lit up when she saw us. "It's nice to see you all here! Let me introduce you to my husband, Hawkeye. Honey, these are the people from the new inn, up by Carter's place."

"Nice to meet y'all," he said, tipping his hat.

"Would you like some goodies?" Birdie asked. "On the house for my new friends."

Birdie gave us each a cupcake with bright blue icing and a small candy bird decorating the top.

"Yum, these are delicious," I said. "Thanks Birdie. Nice to meet you Hawkeye."

We turned away from the booth and nearly walked into Carter. He was standing there with his daughter and her two friends. "You remember my daughter, Duchess, and her friends Selena and Brandy?"

We said hello and chatted with the girls. I wasn't a short person, but all three of them were quite a bit taller than me, with athletic builds. They were in cheerleader sweatshirts, which would explain their fitness levels. All three had their hair in ponytails and I smiled at the three distinctly different shades of their hair: red, blond, and black.

All the girls seemed very sweet, and I thought about Brandy's father, Outlaw Swiftwater, and what Birdie had told us. I wondered if he had anything to do with Randall Ward's demise.

"You girls want cupcakes?" Carter asked them. They nodded and he gave them money. They turned to get into the line forming in front of the booth.

Carter leaned forward toward Emiko. "You have a bit of blue icing right here." He used his thumb to remove the spot of icing off her chin.

Emiko blushed and stammered a thank you. My heart clenched knowing that this budding relationship was soon to hit a brick wall. Or rather, a spinning globe and a room of fog.

"I'm about to take the girls over to see the horses in the barn exhibit hall. Want to join us?"

"I'd love to," said Emiko, while Glo and I shook our heads and declined.

"Is that okay?" said Emiko, looking at me with pleading eyes.

"Sure," I said. "We'll meet you at the gate at eight o'clock."

~ ~ ~

"It's after eight. Where's Emiko?" asked Vee.

The whole group – minus Emiko – was clustered at the front gate. Zell and Moonbeam each held several small stuffed animal game prizes. We were all scanning the crowd for Emiko.

"Umm. She went off with Carter to see the horses," I told them.

"You lost Koko?" laughed Frank. "Paige? Our illustrious organized group leader?"

"I didn't lose her," I said. "I know right where she is."

Frank made a clicking noise. "She's not here. Where she's s'posed to be."

My phone pinged. "It's a text. From Emiko. She says everyone meets in the big field behind the food tents right before sunset. She's heading there now and says she'll meet us. See? She's not lost at all."

By the time we reached the field, several hundred people were already there. We didn't see Emiko, but we did run into Birdie and her family. We chatted with Birdie and Hawkeye while their four kids sat on the grass playing with the dandelions.

"What goes on here?" Glo asked Birdie.

Hawkeye's head turned so fast he almost knocked off his white cowboy hat. "They don't know?" he said.

"Apparently not," laughed Birdie. She turned toward us. "How long have y'all been in town?"

I had to think for a moment. So much had happened it seemed like a month had gone by. "Wow, that's crazy. It's been less than a week, but it seems like so much more."

Birdie chuckled, but it sounded more like a twitter. Perhaps that's where she got her nickname. "It's about to get a whole lot crazier," she said.

The sun was beginning to set. There was a drumbeat followed by a trumpet call, like what's heard at the start of a horse race. It ended with a loud cheer from the crowd.

Birdie, Hawkeye, and their four children began to glow and sparkle. Then there was a loud *pop* and a cloud of dust. When the dust settled, there on the ground before us sat a large blue jay, four small blue jays, and a massive hawk. The two large birds turned to us and bobbed their heads, then the six of them took off in the sky toward the forest behind the field.

All that was left behind was a pile of their clothing on the ground, with a white cowboy hat right on top.

27

One by one, the people around us began to shimmer and glow, then they would pop into a cloud of dust. Animals would emerge from the dust and run or fly off into the wooded hills behind us.

We spotted Daisy and Jeremiah Remlinger on a hill just behind us. Jeremiah stood in front with three other men, hands on hips, looking out at the forest. Daisy and three other women stood behind them. Some of the women held the hands of children. A few teenagers lingered nearby. Suddenly, all as one, the entire group began to shimmer, then came the pop and the dust cloud.

When the dust cleared there were three majestic bucks with impressive antlers standing proudly on the top of the hill. Behind them were three does, a group of smaller deer, and several fawns. The bucks took the lead and the entire herd sprinted off into the woods.

"Oh, my stars!" Moonbeam gushed. "Daisy wasn't shooting deer – she is a deer! She was *protecting* them."

Our heads were spinning trying to take it all in. Everywhere we looked was a pop, a cloud of dust and new animals running, flying, or slithering off into the woods.

"Mom, look," said Forrest, pointing. "Over there. Yuma and Akemi Tanaka – you know, Leaf and Serenity."

We all looked to where Forrest was pointing. We could see the couple. They were looking ahead, pointing, and laughing. We saw the cloud of dust, and then two sleek cougars. They crouched down, setting their sights on a group of rabbits who had just changed and were bounding into the brush. Yuma and Tanaka watched until the rabbits had entered the woods. Then they took off on a sprint.

Sebastian cringed. "Oooh. That's just not right!" He covered his eyes.

"I told you something was up with them. They are not good people ... err ... cougars," said Forrest.

"It looks like you're right, Forrest." I shook my head in disbelief.

We purposely pulled our eyes away from the two cougars who were entering the woods. We scanned the field around us. It seemed the last of the crowd was shifting into animals and taking off toward the freedom of the wilderness.

One small group of animals was dodging the others and heading fast in our direction. As they got closer, we realized that it was four horses. There was a human being riding the largest horse.

"Oh my gosh! Look! It's Emiko!" shrieked Sebastian. "Emiko!" He started waving wildly with both arms.

"That's crazy!" cried Moonbeam. "She doesn't have a saddle – she's bareback." She leaned forward and squinted her eyes. "I don't see any reins either."

The four horses approached. It was indeed Emiko riding the largest horse. She had a grip on his mane, but it appeared that he was doing the navigation. They stopped right in front of us, and Emiko slid down off the large horse. She was flushed and gasping for air.

"That was the most amazing ride I've ever had in my life!" Her entire face was aglow. "You guys will never believe this. Not in a million, zillion years!"

She reached up and petted the horse's neck. He was a beautiful, rich glossy brown and had a deep black tail and mane. The horse leaned down and nuzzled her neck, and she giggled.

"This horse is really Carter!" she announced.

We stared at her and at the horse, our mouths dropped open in shock.

"It's Carter! He shifts into a horse during the changing season festival! Can you believe it!"

We clearly could not believe it.

Emiko walked over to a reddish-chestnut mare. "This is Carter's daughter, Duchess." Then she stood beside a sleek black mustang. "This is Selena. Isn't her coat fabulous?"

We nodded mutely.

With a skip in her step, she put her hand on the remaining horse, a lighter brown mare with a flowing white mane and tail. "This beauty is Brandy.

"Carter explained it all to me. We are in the middle of a community of shifters. They celebrate the times during the year when they are all permitted to shift and run wild in the wilderness. They call it the Changing Season Festival. Get it? It's not about the seasons, it's the people who are changing! Though it really is both, since it often does coincide with the four seasons. We were just lucky enough to be here for a festival!"

Emiko was vibrating with excitement. "And when I ride Carter, I don't need a saddle or reins or anything because he does the driving! I just go along for the ride. Does anyone want to go riding with us? Before the girls changed they offered a ride."

The horses whinnied and lifted their heads. They clearly understood our conversation.

"No, no. That's okay. Thanks anyway," said

Sebastian, backing a few steps away from the horses.

No one else was brave enough to step up for a ride. We all shook our heads.

"You go ahead Emiko," I said. We'll see you at the inn later, okay."

"If you're sure?"

"We are!" said Glo. "You're the only one with riding experience. Go ahead! Have fun."

We stood in the field watching Emiko and the four horses ride off, their manes and her hair flying in the wind. We were now the only ones left standing in a field scattered with piles of discarded clothing.

"This is totally bizarre. I just can't believe it..." said Glo.

"So, let me get this straight," said Frank. "You've entered a murder mystery story by being transported through a book ... your house followed you here ... you're spending time with the most unbelievably wonderful talking cat ... yet you can't believe that shifters exist?"

"Frank, are you a shifter?" Moonbeam asked, looking very closely at his face.

He laughed, a great big belly guffaw. "I wish! I came into the book with you, silly. Remember?"

28

The front door opened, and we could hear the sound of a horse's hooves clopping away down the road. A moment later, Emiko joined us in the kitchen. Her face was flushed, her hair was a mess, and I'd never seen her look happier.

"Hi!" She gave us all a wave.

"Emiko! Did you really ride on Carter the horse or was I dreaming?" asked Moonbeam.

"This whole thing is a dream!" gushed Emiko. "Carter the horse is just as wonderful as Carter the man. It was amazing!"

"He really told you everything before he shifted?" asked Vee.

"Yeah, he did. He said there are rules about who they can tell, but since we live in the neighborhood and since we were at the festival, it was only a matter of minutes before I'd know the truth. I think it's ... mind-blowing-world-altering unbelievably fantastic!"

"So, then, I'm guessing you like him?" Frank drawled.

Everyone laughed and conversation paused when Moonbeam hit the start button on her juicer. Behind her Zell was pouring a bag of tortilla chips into a bowl and Glo was making a pot of coffee. Sebastian was making a cheese tray and Frank was trying to eat the cheese.

When the noise of the blender stopped, Moonbeam said, "This whole thing is mind-blowing. I'm still in a state of shock. Can you believe we've been living in a town filled with people who shift into animals!"

"Did you see the snakes?" said Forrest. "They were the coolest."

"Yeah," said Vee. "The owls were watching them from the tree. I wonder how many people they lose during these festivals?"

"Vee! That's awful!" said Sebastian.

"Well, those cougars sure looked intent on following the rabbits." Vee shrugged. "Natural order of things, circle of life, and all that."

"Maybe there are laws?" I snatched a chip and salsa from Zell's tray. "I mean they have laws about who they can tell, and perhaps laws about when they can shift, so it would make sense that they're not allowed to ... umm ... prey on each other, right?" I crunched the salsa-coated chip, then realized something. I gasped and almost choked on the chip. Sebastian handed me a glass of water.

I slapped the table in front of me. "Now we know why Randall Ward was naked! He shifted!"

All heads turned my way. I was still choking and took another sip of water.

Moonbeam jumped up and down and raised her hand. "I know! It's because he was *an animal* when he entered that trap!"

"Right ..." said Forrest. "The piles of clothes in the field. Because when they shift they leave their clothes behind."

"But why hasn't anyone else shifted except during the festival?" asked Vee.

"Hmmm. Maybe they do?" Forrest looked thoughtful. "I mean, I've seen birds, deer, horses, dogs, cats—"

"So maybe some of them do shift at times other than the festival?"

"I had been stumped how a full-grown man

could fit in that small trap," said Zell, "I thought they must have killed him first and kind of folded and scrunched him in there." She made motions like she was folding and scrunching something. "But luring an animal in there would make a lot more sense."

"Ya don't say?" said Frank.

"What kind of animal do you think he shifts into?" said Sebastian. "Something creepy, I bet."

"A skunk," said Forrest, calmly sipping his smoothie.

"Or a tarantula!" said Moonbeam. "Or maybe a rat, or a worm or—"

"No, Mom. A skunk. Remember how people kept saying Randall Ward was a skunk? We thought they meant like a bad guy kind of skunk, but I bet they meant a skunk kind of skunk."

"You're right, Forrest! Good job!" I enthusiastically complimented him.

"Thanks, Paige." He smiled with pride.

"A skunk would make sense," I agreed. "They are destructive, smelly creatures. They get into garbage, they spread disease, and they're considered an environmental nuisance. That sounds like Randall Ward, to me."

"The shifting aspects of this case can help clarify who the suspects are," said Zell.

"I know it's late and we're all tired, but there's no way I'll sleep." I looked around as everyone nodded. "Who's up for a meeting to review our murder board?"

There was a hearty round of agreement.

"Food, first!" said Zell.

"How about we take our snacks down there with us?" suggested Glo.

Ten minutes later we were all traipsing down the stairs carrying a virtual buffet of snacks and beverages, plus a fresh pot of coffee to keep us all alert.

It took the coffee table plus both end tables shoved together to fit all the food since everyone had grabbed something from the kitchen to add to the offerings.

"Careful not to spill on the furniture!" warned Sebastian.

"Why do you think the chairs have a floral pattern?" said Zell. "Snacking and book clubs have always gone together."

"That's right. I keep forgetting that you've been through many books," said Vee. "Have you ever been in a book with shifters before?"

"Nope, not shifters. Vampires, once. And a ghost or two."

"Seriously?" gasped Moonbeam. "Vampires and ghosts! Can you tell us—"

"Another time," I cut in. We should focus on the case at hand."

I flipped the white board over to the empty side. "Let's list the people we know as possible suspects and what they shift into."

"Good thinking there, Paige-o-paper!" said Frank.

I ignored his inane nickname and began writing names.

"Did anyone see what Cheyenne and Outlaw Swiftwater turned into? I'm assuming horses, like their daughter?"

"Yep, horses," said Emiko. "Carter told me, and then I saw them on our ride."

Everyone piped in and soon we had a list.

"Just because they shift doesn't make them guilty," said Emiko, in a huff.

"Of course not," I said. "But we've only been here a week, we really don't know anything about these people. Let's add motives to the list, based on what we do know."

We agreed that all the neighboring homeowners had the motive of the river pollution. Yuma and Akemi also had the same motive, plus the natural enemy aspect of cougar and skunk. Birdie and her family had no motive that we could tell, except maybe that they were birds, and he was a skunk – a natural enemy, since skunks eat birds. And then we recalled the day we saw Jeremiah and Daisy climbing through the fence onto Randall Wards property looking for their supposed cat.

Randall Ward – Skunk?

Jeremiah & Daisy Remlinger – Deer – river pollution/gardens

Cheyenne and Outlaw Swiftwater – Horses – river pollution/orchard and stables

Carter and Duchess Mahoney – Horses – river pollution/ orchard and stables

Birdie and her four children – Blue Jays – natural enemies

Birdie's husband, Hawkeye – Hawk – natural enemies

Yuma & Akemi Tanaka (Leaf & Serenity) – Cougars – river pollution & natural enemies

"Why would Birdie be on the list?" asked Moonbeam.

"She lives just down the street. A few houses past Daisy's place. Glo and I spotted her kids playing in the yard when we went for a walk. So, they are another river-front neighbor."

"Why would an officer of the law kill someone?" said Emiko. She was sitting stiffly in her seat, with her arms crossed. "And you can't possibly think those lovely teen girls had anything to do with this?"

"We're just listing who we know." Glo tried to calm Emiko down. "The list is very limited. We need to get back into town and see if we can dig up the petition against Randall Ward. Find out who created it, and who's signed it."

"Maybe the town hall would have records?" said Vee.

"They might also have complaints filed against him at the police station," said Emiko. "Maybe Carter would share that information with us."

"Well, he'd likely share it with you, Cupcake," chuckled Frank.

Forrest held up a local newspaper. "I grabbed this from the festival."

"You sly dog!" said Sebastian.

"Don't you mean sly cat?" said Frank. "Dogs are too goofy to be sly. Cats are the sly ones."

"Dogs are not goofy," said Moonbeam. "Merely more honest than cats."

"Hey! Cats are honest. We never pretend not to be sly." Frank's tail twitched.

I cleared my throat and steered us back on track. "What does the newspaper say? Anything in there about the murder?"

"Nothing about the murder, other than a mention of his funeral and stuff."

"We should go!" said Zell.

"There's no date set," said Forrest. "Since it's in the middle of an investigation. They're just having—" He glanced at the paper, "—a memorial service."

"We should go!" said Zell again. "The murderer often goes to the service."

"Good point," I said. "Does it say when or where it is?"

"Nope," said Forrest.

"Okay. Another thing to research in town," I said.

Forrest was leafing through the paper. "Hey, here's something. It's about a horse show. Says that

Cheyenne, Outlaw, and Brandy Swiftwater attended. It was out of town." He read more of the article. "So did Carter's daughter, Duchess, and Selena, too. Details ... details ... ah! A date! It happened the day after we got in the book."

"Aha!" Emiko jumped out of her chair. "They have alibis! You can cross them off the list."

"Right, solid alibi," I agreed. I crossed them off.

"Our list is pretty darn small, and not helpful at all," said Sebastian with a pout. "I hope we can learn something in town."

"You know what," I tapped my finger to my chin. "Even though the neighbors aren't suspects, they did live right next door to the victim. They might have information that would be helpful. I mean, we didn't know Randall Ward, but they did."

"How are we going to get them talking?" asked Vee.

"Let's have a cocktail party! Here at the inn! We can host an open house welcome event," said Glo.

Zell clapped her hands. "How about a Mexican theme? Chips and Salsa! And fajitas!"

Everyone groaned.

"You know what? Zell's right," said Sebastian. "One good gossipy party fueled by margaritas could loosen their tongues."

"Yeah!" said Zell. "Lots of salty chips and a nice cold pitcher with a generous serving of tequila could get them all talking."

We set a plan to invite the neighbors the next morning and then have the open house in the evening. We'd buy party supplies when we went into town.

Emiko let out a huge yawn, which became contagious.

"It's been a long day. We should get to bed," I said.

We plodded up the stairs. When we got to the living room there was a gray tabby cat sitting on our windowsill outside, looking in at us.

"Hey," said Frank. "There's Daisy and Jeremiah's pet. Do you believe his name is Cat? Talk about unimaginative owners."

Leave it to Frank, the neighbor wanderer. That cleared up the so-called fake story of them looking for their lost gray tabby cat named Cat.

29

Glo parked the van a few blocks away from the Mexican restaurant so we wouldn't have to wrestle Zell away from the place. We did, however, get talked into stopping at the bakery before we made our way to the town hall. At least Frank had stayed at home to nap, so we had one less peanut in the gallery.

"Hello, neighbors!" Birdie wiped her hands on a towel and gave us a wave. "Quite the festival yesterday, right? Ahhh. So nice to get in a good fly."

"It was a beautiful day for it," said Zell, as if she'd lived with bird shifters all her life. Maybe after I'd been in books with vampires and ghosts I'd be so unflappable. But probably not. Of course, at eighty years old she had a few years more experience with life than I did. And she certainly embraced every experience.

"I have some lovely Birdie's Bits today." She pulled out the tray of crumb-filled muffin papers and we all reached for a sample.

"We're in town for supplies," said Glo. "We're having an open house tonight at the inn. A Mexican food fiesta of sorts. Can you and Hawkeye join us? You can bring the kids, if you'd like."

"I'll take the date-night, thank you very much! I know Hawkeye will love to come. I'll ask his brother to stay with the kids. They love when he's over. He tends to fall asleep in front of the TV and they get away with eating too much junk food! Actually, he's with them already today, since Hawkeye and I are both working, so I'll just ask if he can stay later. At least I won't have to worry about making dinner for the band," she laughed.

"The band?" I asked.

"That's what you call a group of Blue Jays."

"Oh! Wow. Cool." I was still absorbing the fact that this blue-haired woman was also a bird. "I'm glad you two can make it tonight." I took a bite from my muffin cup. "Yum. What's in here today?"

"Poppy seed muffins and toasted pumpkin seed bread."

I smiled at that. Suddenly the seeds and crumbs made all the sense in the world.

"Hey, Birdie. Do you happen to know who started the petition against Randall Ward for the river pollution?"

"Oh, that horrible, horrible man." She kind of puffed up and shivered.

I recognized the movement, since I had a parakeet when I was a child that used to puff up like that when it was anxious, stressed, or happy.

"I think it was those folks who do the petitions outside the market. Have you ever seen them there? Leaf and Harmony."

"It's Leaf and Serenity," said Moonbeam, stepping closer. "That makes sense since petitions are their thing. Any idea where we can get a copy? Is it online you think?"

"They're old school, so I doubt it's online. I saw them in front of the market yesterday morning. Maybe they'll be there again."

"Thanks. We have shopping to do, so we'll check it out," said Moonbeam. "I'll take one of those poppy seed muffins and a slice of the toasted seed bread, please."

Birdie packed up Moonbeam's order, then made her way through the group handing over paper bags and small white boxes filled with goodies.

~ ~ ~

"There they are!" said Sebastian. He started marching over to the folding table in front of the market.

"Sebastian! A word, please?" I pulled him aside and whispered. "Let Moonbeam do it. She talks their language. Let's go in the market and start shopping so they don't get overwhelmed by our group."

Moonbeam was standing next to us and understood the assignment. She nodded briskly and pulled her canvas bag up on her shoulder. Then she meandered slowly to the petitioner's table. We walked past and into the market.

We were mulling over the vast choices of salsa when Moonbeam joined up with us. She looked over her shoulder and out the window to be sure Leaf and Serenity were still outside.

"They know about the petition," she said. "They told me that they signed it, but they didn't instigate it. Though they would have if no one else jumped on it. They suggested going to the town hall, as people often leave a copy there for people to come by and sign."

"Excellent!" I patted her on the arm. "Good recon, Moonbeam."

"Thanks, Paige! Now, I'm going to gather up some tomatoes, peppers, onions, lime, and cilantro. None of this jarred salsa, folks." She waved her hand dismissively toward the rows of salsa jars. We all followed her to the produce department.

~ ~ ~

After packing up our groceries in the van, we stopped by the town hall.

"Will they ask us why we want to know about the petition?" asked Forrest. "Seems weird to just walk in and want to see it."

"We just tell them we're helping to investigate the murder," said Zell. "Most of these people don't think for themselves – they're too one dimensional." She laughed heartily. "Get it? Cuz they're characters in a book." She kept laughing at her own joke. One by one, the humor of it hit us until we were all chuckling.

"To be honest, they seem to be more like four-dimensional," said Forrest. "Maybe even extraterrestrial."

"Whoa, slow down there boy. Our brains are already in a tizzy. No need to stir the pot," said Sebastian.

"Oh, my!" said Moonbeam. "I'd never even thought of it like that."

"Imagine the possibilities!" said Vee, looking intrigued.

We tabled the topic for another day and went into the town hall building. As Zell suggested, the clerk had no problem going into the file drawer to get the document for us. The clerk showed us the petition.

"It looks like it's been signed by a couple hundred people!" I gasped.

Glo looked over my shoulder at the paper. "Wow, that's a lot of names!"

"That filthy skunk was polluting the heck out of

our river. Of course everybody would sign it! It was about to be filed as a formal document when … umm … you know." Her face scrunched into a grimace.

"Oh. Right. Do you know who filed the original petition?" asked Glo.

"Let me check."

The clerk came back. "I'm afraid it was filed anonymously. We don't normally allow that, but given that the river pollution was such a big deal they let this one proceed."

"Okay, thanks for checking," I said. "We appreciate your time."

~ ~ ~

We felt like our trip into town was helpful that day. It was like we were finally making progress in figuring out this mystery. While there were hundreds of people who signed the petition, we still didn't know who instigated it, but we were going to set Forrest and Emiko to researching it when we got home.

Zell was nodding off in the back seat. We were all still tired from the crazy few days we'd had.

As we drove down our street, we passed Birdie's house. Her four blue-haired children were playing in the vast front yard. They were laughing and running around.

"They're throwing colorful balls in the air. No, wait. It actually looks like a wild game of tag, but they're tossing balls at each other," said Moonbeam, laughing.

"No. Not balls," said Emiko. "Colorful plastic Easter eggs."

"What?!" gasped Sebastian. "Did you say plastic Easter eggs?"

"Holeee Toledo!" Glo gasped.

"No way," said Forrest.

"Keep driving," I said to Glo. "Get past where they can see us."

"Here's what we need to do," said Zell, popping to life in the back seat. "Someone needs to go back there and do some recon. Remember, Birdie said her brother-in-law is babysitting and he falls asleep by the TV. The kids are busy, they won't notice. It's a perfect time to check it out."

"Are you out of your—" I started to say.

"That's a crazy—" started Emiko.

"I'll do it!" said Sebastian and Vee both together. They bumped fists.

"Oh, my! You two are so brave!" breathed Moonbeam.

Sebastian looked intense. Vee looked relaxed and ... entertained? I guess she finally internalized the fact that we were in a mystery book.

"What?" She caught Emiko's eye. "It's time to be an investigator."

Sebastian and Vee exited the van and went back down the street toward the house. They were attempting to stick to the bushes as they went. They rustled leaves and snapped branches along the way. They were about as inconspicuous as a monkey in a sand dune.

We waited in the van. I was ticking off the minutes along with my racing heartbeat. Finally, I couldn't take it any longer.

"I'm going to try to see what they're up to."

"Going with you!" said Glo, following me out of

the van.

"Be careful!" yelled Moonbeam.

We walked slowly down the road until Birdie's house came into view.

Glo grabbed my arm and whispered, "They're playing with the kids in the front yard!"

"Are you kidding me?" Sure enough, they were in the middle of the four blue-haired children. "Did the kids catch them spying, you think?"

"No – it looks like they're playing tag. No, wait. It's hide-and-seek," said Glo. "One of the kids is leaning on a tree with his eyes closed. Vee and Sebastian just ran toward the back of the house!"

"Okay," I said. "Maybe this will work!"

Glo and I returned to the van to tell everyone what was happening. When we got back, Moonbeam, Emiko, and Zell were sitting on the grass playing cards. Forrest had the front seat tilted back and was scrolling on his phone. We sat down on the grass and waited.

It was quite a while, then we finally spotted Vee and Sebastian running back toward us, not even attempting to be discrete.

Sebastian was breathing heavy from the run. "They ... have ... a box." He put his hands on his knees and bent over to catch his breath. "Vee ... tell ... them."

"No, you go ahead, Sebastian. We'll wait." Vee wasn't breathing heavy at all, but I realized she was being kind. She wanted Sebastian to have his moment.

"Tell us!" shouted Moonbeam, Forrest, and Glo in unison.

Sebastian sucked in a deep breath and stood back up with his hands on his hips.

"There is a box!" he huffed.

"A box," said Zell. "Oooo. Front page news."

"No, no! Listen!" He held a hand to his chest, trying to catch his breath. "The kids have a fort in the back yard." Sebastian leaned against the van and took another deep breath. "It's behind their garage partially hidden in the bushes. It's made from a bunch of old boxes."

Zell rolled her eyes. "Ohhh! Not just one box, but a bunch of them!"

Sebastian's eyes got big and round. "One of the boxes is from an animal trap. What did you call it, Moonbeam?"

"A wire one-door animal trap?"

"Yeah, that's it! It's the box from the trap that we found the dead guy in!"

30

My hands were shaking when I called Carter. I tried to stay calm when I explained what Sebastian and Vee had found. I added the fact that the children were playing with colorful plastic Easter eggs. He told us to stay put at the van. He was going to call this into his sergeant.

"Carter said they'd be here as quick as possible. We're supposed to stay at the van."

"It's like we're on a stakeout!" said Zell.

"Not quite," said Vee, laughing.

It wasn't long before two cars came up the road. They weren't police cars, though. Both cars pulled into the driveway. We watched as Birdie and Hawkeye got out of their cars. They embraced in the driveway and began to chat as they went into the house. They were home from work.

Minutes later a police car drove past us.

"There's no way I'm sittin' here," said Zell. "We found the evidence. Sorry—" she looked over at Sebastian with a wide grin and a wink. "I mean, Sebastian and Vee found the evidence, so we ought to be over there."

Zell began to march down the street, her arms pumping in time with her feet. Of course, we all followed. When we reached the house, Carter and a man in a police uniform, the sergeant we assumed, were knocking at the front door.

"We should stay here, because it's a respectful

distance away," said Zell.

"You mean stay here because you don't want them to tell us to leave," said Vee.

"That sounds more like Zell," said Moonbeam.

"Shhh!" Emiko pointed at the house where Hawkeye had just come outside. "Quiet, so we can hear."

"Afternoon, Carter," said Hawkeye.

"Good afternoon, Hawkeye. This is officer O'Donnell."

Hawkeye nodded. "What brings you here?"

"We got a tip about something in your backyard. Mind if we check it out?"

"Can't imagine what it is, but sure."

Carter, the sergeant, and Hawkeye went around the front of the house and headed to the back yard. We stayed a bit behind, but within hearing distance. Carter glanced at us but didn't shoo us away.

"What's this?" Carter asked, pointing to the fort.

Hawkeye looked confused. "It's my kids' fort. You know how kids are. Making forts out of whatever they can find around. Healthy play. What's this about? Do I need a permit?" he chuckled.

Carter knelt on the grass and pointed to the animal cage box. "This box right here. Where'd it come from?"

"I have no idea," said Hawkeye.

Carter leaned closer and examined the box. "It's got a shipping label with your address on it."

"No clue," said Hawkeye, shrugging his shoulders.

Carter stuck his head inside the fort, then stood up and faced Hawkeye.

"There's a box of plastic Easter eggs in there."

"Yeah, so? The kids play with those. Left over from last Easter."

The sergeant stepped forward toward Hawkeye. "We'll need to ask you to come to the station and answer some questions, sir."

"Questions about what? My kids' fort is on my own property."

"Exactly," said Officer O'Donnell. "We have questions about the animal trap."

Birdie came out the back door. She took one look at Carter and the sergeant and began to wring her hands. "What's happening?"

"It's okay, honey. They have some questions about this animal trap box," said Hawkeye. "Do you know where the kids got it?"

"I don't know. Maybe the neighbors? They're always giving stuff to the kids."

"It's got a label with your address on it," said Carter.

"Really? That's very odd." She laughed uncomfortably. "Maybe a mistake? I didn't buy a trap, did you Hawkeye? A simple mistake, I'm sure."

"It's not a simple mistake," said Carter. "This box may be evidence in a murder investigation."

"Murder!" squeaked Birdie.

Carter turned to Hawkeye. "Can you come with us to the station for questioning?"

"I don't understand why. We've done nothing wrong. You can't force me to go in with no grounds. Can't you ask me your questions right here?"

"I'm afraid we do need you to come in. You're right, we can't make you. I'd have to get a court order. But it would be easier if you'd just come on down and chat with us."

Birdie stepped closer to her husband and reached up to put her hand on his arm. "Sweetheart, you don't have to go. They can't make you!"

"Hush, honey. I got this. I'll just go chat with them. Find out what this is all about."

We followed at a distance as they approached the police car. Birdie looked panicked as Carter opened the door and Hawkeye started to get in.

Birdie let out a horrific wail, and we all ran over to her.

"Birdie! We're here for you," said Moonbeam, reaching out to the panicked woman.

Birdie dodged Moonbeam and the rest of the group.

"No!" she yelled, running toward the men. "Carter! Hawkeye doesn't know anything about this!"

Carter walked up close to Birdie. "We're just trying to get to the bottom of this."

"I know what happened!" Birdie cried.

"What do you mean?" asked Hawkeye, staring at his wife.

Birdie moved to stand in front of her husband. She was shaking. She took his hand in both of hers.

"It was that horrible, frightening Randall Ward! He's been shifting out of season and stalking our children! I kept seeing him in the yard. He'd wait 'til they came home from school and just sit there in his skunk form watching them. Watching them and waiting."

"What?" said Hawkeye. "Why didn't you tell me? Why didn't you report him?

"I was going to, but I was scared! And ... the kids! They started shifting when you weren't home. I knew you'd be furious with them. And if anyone found out, they would be in trouble for shifting out of season, and so would we! I kept finding them in the front yard shifted. I was petrified that the skunk was going to ... to ... eat them!"

"What are you saying?" Hawkeye stood toe to toe with his wife. She looked up at him. "I got rid of him."

The sergeant stepped forward toward Birdie, as if to arrest her, but Carter put his hand out to stop him. "Sir, can you give her time to talk to her husband? I'll remain at her side."

The sergeant nodded and walked over to stand beside the police car. He reached in for his mic and we could hear his voice as he spoke over his radio.

"Thanks, Carter," said Hawkeye. "Birdie, honey. Tell me what you've done."

We sat in rapt attention as Birdie told her story. She flapped her arms as she spoke and occasionally, she puffed up like my parakeet. I wondered if she was anxious, stressed, or maybe even happy that she'd protected her children and eliminated the skunk.

"It's his own fault," she was saying to Hawkeye and Carter. "I asked him to get off our property. I said I'd turn him in for off-season shifting. I threatened to call the police. He just laughed and kept coming back. He said—" She choked up and swallowed. "He said baby birds were his favorite treat!"

Hawkeye gasped. "He said that to you?"

She nodded and hung her head. Her husband put his finger under her chin and lifted up her face. There were tears rolling down her cheeks.

"Tell me," he said gently.

Carter lifted up his phone, turning it to show Hawkeye the audio record button. Hawkeye gave a brisk nod.

"I ordered the trap. It came while you were at work. I put it together."

"Why were the kids' toy eggs in there?" Hawkeye looked confused.

"They were playing while I put it together. They didn't know what it was for. They kept trying to toss eggs into the door. It was dark, and I forgot to take the eggs out." She looked glassy eyed. "I was distracted."

"Go on," Hawkeye said. I was impressed that his voice was so kind.

"I doused some food with rodent poison. I took everything over to Randall Ward's house one night when I worked late at the bakery. I watched from outside. When he turned out the lights and went to sleep, I dragged the trap through his yard. I threw the poisoned food it in the trap, I left it there. End of story."

"Except it wasn't the end, Birdie," said Carter. "The skunk shifted back into a dead man in that cage."

Birdie nodded. "I know." But then she looked up at her husband again and with a wicked smile on her face said, "Good riddance to him."

Hawkeye pulled his wife into his arms and squeezed her tight. "I know you were protecting our babies. I love you for that."

A few minutes later Carter approached the couple. "Birdie, can you come with me now?"

"Can I get my purse?" she asked.

"Certainly." Carter escorted her into the house.

Hawkeye faced us. "Thanks for being here. You're good friends," he said. Then he turned and went into the house.

31

We prepared the feast for our Mexican-themed dinner party, but the mood was anything but fiesta. We were glad the case was solved, but we were heartbroken that the murderer was Birdie.

"She's such a sweet little lady!" said Sebastian as he chopped onions for the salsa. "And I am not crying – it's the onions."

"Yeah, because I know that's why you requested onion-chopping duty," said Vee. "But it's okay Sebastian. We're all sad about Birdie."

In a rare moment of physical affection, she went over and gave him a big hug from behind. That just made his onion-chopping tears flow harder.

"It's tragic that she was just protecting her four children, and now they'll be without a mother as she sits in prison," said Glo.

"The book ain't over yet," said Zell, busy opening the two jars of salsa that she bought behind Moonbeam's back.

"But she confessed. She even told the whole story in front of two officers and witnesses." I pointed out the hard facts. "She murdered a man in cold blood. Of course she'll be in prison – for a long time, I expect. Those little birds will grow up without their mother."

"I didn't realize we'd be in such a sad book," said Moonbeam.

"Murder mysteries don't have happy endings for everyone," said Frank. "For that you have to join the Romance Book Club."

"Is there such a thing?" Glo asked, her eyes

shining.

"Heck if I know." Frank jumped up on the counter next to the packages of halibut. "Can somebody open these packages? I think I should sample the fish to be sure its fresh."

Moonbeam snickered as she opened a package and placed a few pieces of fish on a plate for Frank.

"Who would have guessed? Instead of a fact-finding event our dinner has turned into a farewell party," said Moonbeam as she began to dip the fish into her homemade breading.

The doorbell gonged. "Somebody's early," Glo said as she went to answer the door.

Glo returned to the kitchen with Carter.

"Hello, Carter!" said Moonbeam. "Want to help?"

"Sure thing," he said. He removed his hat and hung it on the back of a chair and walked to the sink and washed his hands. Then he turned to Moonbeam and saluted her. "Reporting for duty."

Moonbeam put a bowl of tomatoes, a cutting board, and a knife in front of him. "Think you can handle this?"

He answered by picking up three of the tomatoes and juggling them.

Moonbeam gasped, and the group burst out in laughter. He was quite talented, and not a single tomato fell. I could tell we all enjoyed having a change in the mood, but Sebastian was still obsessing.

"How is poor Birdie doing?" asked Sebastian. "She must be wrecked with the knowledge she'll be leaving those sweet children she loves so much."

"Why?" said Carter, looking confused. "Where's she going?"

"Umm. Prison?" said Sebastian.

"Prison? Oh, Sebastian, no!"

"But we saw you haul her off to jail!"

"We were bringing her in for her official statement. Sorry folks. Wasn't thinking that y'all are new here and probably don't know how our legal system works. Sure, it's a tough situation, but our laws are quite specific.

"To manage a shifting community the rules are precise and known by all. They are crystal clear. Shifting out of season is forbidden. If you shift out of season, then human laws don't apply to you. Your natural animal form rules take precedence. That makes this a human act against a skunk, not another human being. We have a different set of laws that protect everyone in their animal form during the changing seasons, as well. Otherwise, we'd have cougars eating rabbits and owls eating snakes."

"Or skunks eating baby birds," added Zell.

"That's correct, Zell. Birdie entrapped him when he was a skunk, not a human. He was shifting out of season. His skunk form had become an environmental nuisance by polluting the river. Numerous attempts had been made previously to stop the activity, including Birdie's petition that had been signed by several hundred residents. Therefore, she was permitted to dispose of the pest. Birdie didn't kill a human. She killed a skunk. There will be no charges pressed against Birdie."

"No charges? How can that law apply if Birdie knew she was killing a man?" asked Emiko.

"Because it makes sense." Carter smiled at her. "In big cities folks tend to lose sight of common sense. In our town, you apply the laws to make sure the right thing happens."

"Bravo!" said Vee. "A community with their heads on straight. How refreshing."

"So then, the mystery is solved, the bad guy is dead, and Birdie is happy at home," I said. "This story does have a happy ending!"

"Let the party commence!" said Glo turning on a track of fiesta party music.

Our neighbors arrived one by one, each one bearing a small gift for the inn. Carter's daughter, Duchess, and her friends, Selena and Brandy, gave us a ceramic statue of a group of horses in front of a barn. Glo placed it on the fireplace mantle in a position of honor.

Jeremiah and Daisy gave us a handmade lamp – the base made from a gorgeous deer antler. "Naturally shed, of course." She smiled and winked at us, reminding us that at first we thought she had shot the deer to get her collection of antlers. Obviously, we were very wrong about that.

The door gong alerted us to more guests arriving. Zell opened the door to Birdie and Hawkeye. The group surrounded her with hugs and kind words. She was glowing a rosy pink that set off her bright blue hair beautifully. Hawkeye presented us with a painting of a blue sky with a sprinkling of white clouds. Across the sky flew a large blue jay, four small blue jays, and a large hawk.

"This is gorgeous!" said Glo. "Thank you so much."

"Yeah, my sweet Birdie is a talented painter," said Hawkeye.

"Well, how about that," said Zell. "Talented baker, painter, mother-of-the-year, and superhero, all rolled up into a pretty blue bird!" She began to clap.

Everyone joined in and we gave Birdie an enthusiastic round of applause.

Glo turned up the fiesta music and we danced, laughed, talked, and filled ourselves up from the incredible buffet of food.

Far too soon our collection of new friends was saying goodbye and stepping out into the crisp, clear evening. They began walking down the street toward their own homes. Emiko followed them outside. She and Carter sat on the porch swing holding hands, saying a private farewell. I quietly closed the door.

"It's hard to know we'll never see them again. It's amazing how you can get to know people in such a short time."

"'Every adventure is a lifetime of fun.' That's what GeeGee used to say." Zell came up and put an arm around my waist. "You get used to it, honey."

When Emiko came back inside her eyes were red and her face downcast. She held up a hand before anyone could speak. "Please. No one say anything."

We nodded in silence.

"Okay troops! That'll be the ending, I s'pose," said Frank. "Time to head downstairs to the library!"

32

We were gathered in the library. The leftovers from the party were covering the coffee table, since Zell insisted that we bring them down with us.

"Now what?" I turned to Zell and Frank, our two experienced travelers who were more intent on picking through the leftovers than explaining the process of returning home.

"Huh?" asked Frank through a mouthful of leftover fish.

"What's the deal?" asked Vee.

"No deal," said Frank.

"How do we get home?" I asked.

"Don't know. It just happens," said Zell.

"What do you usually do when you come downstairs after the mystery is solved? Other than eat the leftovers," said Glo with a laugh, as she reached for a cinnamon-covered churro.

"Ah! We always finish up the murder board. Maybe that's important?" said Zell.

"Maybe? Maybe! After all these years you don't know for sure?" Sebastian shook his head in disbelief.

"You people are far too rigid. Got to loosen up," said Frank. "Be more Zen and cat-like."

"*You* are the most un-Zen-like cat I've ever met," said Moonbeam.

"And proud of it!" Frank boasted.

I rolled the murder board in front of the group. I took a blue marker and wrote Birdie's name and circled it. I drew an arrow from her name to Randall Ward, Victim. At the top of the board, I wrote: *Mystery Solved.*

I sat down on my chair.

"Look!" said Glo, pointing at the antique globe on the brass stand.

The globe began to glow a brilliant golden hue. It started to slowly spin, then whirled faster and faster. The carpet beneath us turned into a blanket of mist which grew higher and thicker as it enveloped the entire room in a dense white fog. We could no longer see the room or each other.

In minutes, the fog began to dissipate until the air was clear again.

"That's it?" asked Glo. "How do we know if we're home?"

"Well, the books, for one," said Zell, pointing at a neat stack of eight books on the table in front of us.

I untied the twine and opened the top book to the last page. "It says, *The End*!" I held up the book and everyone cheered.

"Now we have to go upstairs and look out the windows," said Frank. "Make sure we're home."

There was no slow trudge up the stairs this time. It was a stampede of footfalls as we all ran up the stairs as fast as we could go.

Glo was in the lead. She reached the top of the stairs and flung open the door.

"Whooo hooo!" she yelled. "We're home!"

Everyone was shouting and jumping up and down, laughing and hugging each other.

"We did it!" said Sebastian. Then he started to sing, "We are the champions, my friend…"

Everyone joined in. "We are the champions! We are the champions! No time for losers 'cause we are the champions! Of the world!"

I was twirling around the room with Glo, our elbows joined as we spun. Then Glo abruptly stopped. She pointed to the sofa. Emiko wasn't joining in the celebration. She was sitting forlornly by herself. I thought about how she had hung on every word Carter said with a dreamy look in her eye. Even though we'd only been there a week, she had fallen hard. It was heartbreaking to know that they would be pulled apart before they even had a chance to begin.

Zell and Frank were the last ones to notice as they were too busy hooting and dancing.

"Lookee here," said Frank, elbowing Zell.

"Think we have us a winner!" said Zell.

"What are you talking about?" I was horrified at their nonchalant response to Emiko's heartbreak.

"Looks like Emiko has found her book!" said Zell.

"What are you saying?" I asked.

"Back downstairs!" hooted Zell.

She and Frank took off down the stairs to the library. We all followed in a cloud of absolute confusion.

Zell went over to the display case that held the antique Underwood typewriter. She opened up the front of the glass case. "Can I have a chair, please?" she said.

Vee moved one of the chairs over in front of the typewriter. Zell cracked her knuckles and poised her fingers over the keyboard.

"Now, what do we say?" she asked.

"Say what? To whom? What the heck are you doing?" asked Sebastian.

"Oh, geeze, Zell. We didn't tell them!" said Frank.

"What a pair of ninnies we are. No wonder Emiko's such a sad sack," laughed Zell.

"Well, don't write that down!" said Frank.

"'Course not, you goofball. That would be a bad place to start."

"What. Are. You. Doing?!" hollered Vee.

Instead of answering her, Zell turned to Emiko who stood silently at the back of the group.

"Emiko, sweetheart. Have you found your one true love?" Zell asked her.

Emiko nodded solemnly.

"Do you wish you could go back and stay there with him?" Zell asked.

"More than anything in the world," said Emiko.

"Got any family here?"

"Why do you ask?" Emiko looked confused.

"Just answer the question," said Zell. "Family?"

"I don't," said Emiko. "My parents passed years ago. I'm an only child."

"Well, then. We use this enchanted typewriter to write you into the story. And then poof!"

"Poof?" I repeated. "What do you mean poof?"

"I got this," said Frank. He climbed up on top of the cabinet and cleared his throat. He looked around to make sure everyone was paying attention. Believe me, we were.

"When you find your book. The place you want to be forever. You use this typewriter to add a last chapter. You write yourself into the story. Then ... poof!"

"Again with the poof!" said Vee. "Say it in English."

"You're in the book!" said Zell and Frank in unison.

"Forever and ever," said Zell.

"And they lived happily ever after," said Frank, putting both paws under his chin, batting his eyelashes, and giving us a dreamy expression.

"You ready to go, Koko?" asked Zell.

Emiko threw her hands in the air and squealed. "Yes, yes, yes!"

"Okay, then. Let's get to it," said Zell.

"How long does it have to be? How much detail do we include?" I asked.

"It can be a few lines, really. You don't want to force it or control it," Zell explained. "Just send her back so they can create their own story together."

We all clustered around the typewriter, everyone adding their opinion. We ended up with a simple, but effective few lines. It wasn't a chapter, but Zell assured us that it was all that was needed.

Carter and Emiko sat on the porch swing holding hands. They talked about the adventure they'd had, and the growing feelings of love they shared for each other. "Will you be my wife?" Carter asked. "Will you stay with me forever?"

"Yes," breathed Emiko.

Carter took her in his arms and promised her a lifetime of happiness.

Zell looked at Emiko, "Is that good?"

"Very good," she said, with a shy smile.

"Okay, then. Everybody say goodbye to Emiko," announced Frank.

We all hugged her, told her how happy we were for her and Carter. We wished her well.

Zell typed, *The End.*

The globe took on its golden hue, sparkles surrounding it. Once again, the room filled with fog. When the fog lifted, our friend Emiko was gone.

Glo opened a copy of the mystery book and flipped to the back. There on the last page was our new ending.

33

Glo added another log to the fire and used a stick to shift the wood around. There was already a blaze hot enough for us to roast our marshmallows. Zell, of course, was the first one to make a s'more and was eating it with gusto.

We'd moved all the Adirondack chairs to circle the fire pit and turned on the twinkle lights that brought the yard alive in the twilight. As amazing as our mystery book adventure had been, it was nice to be home. It was even nicer because Glo and I were sharing our new inn with this amazing group of friends. Everyone had decided to stay for the night so that we could decompress and discuss our journey.

Vee looked out over the lake. "What a great spot. Peaceful."

"Not itching to hit the road on your bike?" asked Glo.

"Think I'm all filled up on adventure, right now," Vee laughed. "Feels good to just sit."

"Hey, Zell." I drew her attention away from the chocolate and marshmallows.

"Huh?"

"How long has the book club been in existence? Did GeeGee start it?"

"Oh, gosh no! The club was started by the American Indians way back before mystery books were even in print. At that point it was oral stories. They have a rich tradition built on stories passed down through generations, you know. Ever wondered why they include so much detail? Why they feel so real?"

"Wow. That's incredible," gushed Moonbeam. "Can you go back into those old stories?"

Forrest looked up from his phone. He was intrigued by that idea, too. Like mother, like son, I guessed.

"Don't know. Never tried. The group tends toward modern-day settings. It's enough to keep up with the story without having to adapt to a whole new century."

Moonbeam chuckled. "Yeah, what would Forrest do without his phone?"

Forrest smirked at his mother and shrugged, but I could see the glow from his phone screen on his lap.

"Do you want to stay in the club, Forrest?" Moonbeam asked. "You don't have to, you know."

"Yeah. I want to, Mom. It's cool."

"That's great!" I gave him a thumbs up. "I'm glad you liked it. You were very helpful, you know."

"Thanks, Paige." Forrest smiled and placed a toasted marshmallow on a paper plate. He leaned down and put it in front of Frank.

Frank sniffed the treat. "Mmmm. Sugar at its finest." He dug right in for a taste, lifting his head to display a sticky white mustache. "If you rent out the rooms in off-season make sure the folks like s'mores."

"Oh! I hadn't thought of that. You all go home when we're here – back to your real homes, right?"

"Yup!" said Zell. "GeeGee used those Airbnb and VRBO sites to rent out the rooms in between books. That's when we catch our breath, have some meetings, and decide on the next book."

"We still have weekly meetings?" asked Moonbeam.

"Well, yeah!" said Zell. "A potluck. Every week. With chips and salsa."

"Zelda!" scolded Frank. He looked around the

group. "We do not have chips and salsa every week."

"We should," she mumbled.

"Sounds fun!" said Glo. "And I like chips and salsa." She smiled warmly at Zell who lifted her s'more in a silent toast.

"I still can't believe that Emiko went back into the book," said Vee. "That's trippy."

"Happens to everybody eventually," said Zell. "Though I still haven't found mine." She gestured with her marshmallow stick. "Ever hopeful, though!"

"You mean other members have gone into books?" Sebastian was breathless with the idea.

"Oh, yeah, sure," said Zell. "That's what happened to all the previous group members. They found their books and left us."

"They went into books! And stayed there?" Forrest had totally abandoned his phone now.

"Yup!" said Frank. "That's how it works. When you find your book, you write yourself into it and there you go."

I stood up so abruptly that I dropped my marshmallow on the ground. "Wait! Are you saying GeeGee isn't dead?!"

"Geeze Louise," said Zell. "Did I ever say GeeGee was dead? I remember distinctly I said, 'She's in a better place.'"

"A book is the better place?"

"Of course the book is the better place. Where else would she be?" said Frank.

"But she left us the house in her will!"

"She wouldn't just leave willy-nilly," said Zell. "She was a planner. She wanted you two to experience the magic."

"That is the most extraordinary thing I've ever heard." I sucked in a breath and shook my head. "GeeGee is living in a book."

"Yep, you got it right. You're a smart one, Paige. Your GeeGee found a book she loved. We wrote her a really great ending and there she went." Zell grinned and fluttered her hands in the air. "Poof!"

The End . . . for now.

What happens next?

The *Magical Mystery Book Club* series continues with more adventures in book two, *Vampires and Villains*.

The gang agrees on their next book journey which takes place on a cruise ship bound for Hawaii. Problem is, they were so excited about the cruising idea that they didn't read the entire blurb on the back of the book. ("It was entirely too long," explains Zell.) Once on the ship, they meet a charming likeable man who blends seamlessly into their motley group. Too bad they don't know why he's so scarce during the day but shows up to join them every evening for dinner, drinks, and a show. When a body shows up on board, their new friend is labeled a suspect. Can they help him out by finding the real murderer? Or ... is he the real murderer? The book club will need to solve the case to get off the ship, out of the book, and back to their home.

Follow me and stay informed about new releases, contests, and special offers.

Sign up for my mailing list here: https://www.nocrysolution.com/mailing-list
Goodreads: https://www.goodreads.com/series/302365-destiny-falls-mystery-magic
Facebook: https://www.facebook.com/DestinyFallsMysteryandMagic
Instagram: https://www.instagram.com/

destinyfallsmystery
BookBub: https://www.bookbub.com/authors/elizabeth-pantley

Thank you for hanging out with the Magical Mystery Book Club!

I hope you enjoyed this book as much as I enjoyed writing it. My husband tells everyone that I skip to work every morning, and he's right. People say find a job you love, and you'll never work a day in your life. Writing these enchanting stories is what I love.

If you enjoyed this book, please consider writing a review on Amazon, Goodreads, BookBub, or another book site. Reviews are the very best way to say thank you to an author for a fun experience. They are also the fuel that feeds the next tale. I appreciate your support.

Just a warning.
Be careful about reading the first page
of the next book out loud.
Only kidding. You're safe. I think.
See you next time!
~ Elizabeth

Want to read more fun mystery books by Elizabeth Pantley?

Check these out!

Magical Mystery Book Club

Shifting and Shenanigans
Vampires and Villains
Cowboys and Chaos
Bakeries and Buffoonery

Destiny Falls Mystery and Magic

Falling into Magic
The Disappearance of Emily
The Ghost Camper's Tall Tales
Witches, Spiders, and Schemes
Jousting and Justice
Old Bones and Ice Cream Cones

Visit my page at Amazon to read about all my other books.

https://www.amazon.com/Elizabeth-Pantley/e/B000APFU6Y

Made in the USA
Coppell, TX
08 March 2023

13986816R00132